Ten Thousand Rocks

by NDIRANGU GITHAIGA

DEDICATION

For the fine citizens of Hampton Roads

ACKNOWLEDGEMENTS

My heartfelt gratitude goes to my wife and kids for walking with me through this continuing journey of discovery. And to Maitũ and my fellow members of Mbarĩ ya Githaiga—thank you for your incredible support on so many levels. Many thanks to my editor, Joslyn Pine, for your excellent insights and being such a joy to work with. And as always, thanks to Adonai, the source of all beautiful stories.

"Here is the sea, great and wide, which teems with creatures innumerable, living things both small and great. There go the ships, and Leviathan, which you formed to play in it." Psalm 104: 25 – 26

Prologue

THAT PARTICULAR DAY was a little too hot—even for August—so that walking barefoot on the sand quickly became uncomfortable. A steady breeze was coming off the ocean, sending a motley array of multicolored kites soaring gracefully above the shoreline, their owners craning their necks as they gently pulled on the strings below, stepping back and forth to avoid getting their kites entangled. Foamy breakers rippled through the emerald-green surface of the water and crawled rhythmically onto the sand, only to be dragged back into the sea, occasionally leveling a sandcastle a child had been building only moments before. Out on the horizon, far beyond where the brave and foolhardy swimmers frolicked, large ships inched across the horizon over the shimmering indigo surface.

Will spotted the familiar figure emerging from among the row of hotels and apartments that sat back about fifty yards from the beachgoers who'd settled farthest from the shore. The old man shuffled along casually yet purposefully, a stooped figure wearing a misshapen straw hat, a worn-out blazer and mid-calf-length pants that had taken on a faded color somewhere between gray and brown after years of constant use.

Making his way between the broken rows of sunscreen-slathered loungers and rapturous children who cavorted in the sand, he reached the water's edge and waded in, still in his sandals, until the water reached the middle of his thighs. Next, he lifted his right arm and deftly tossed an egg-sized object into the water, then turned around and made his way back, disappearing into the same gap between the buildings he'd materialized from.

Will pointed and said to Laura, "You see that guy?"

"Yes," Laura said, raising her sunglasses to look, and squinting from the sun's glare.

"He comes here every single day. Ask anyone who comes to the beach around this time in the afternoon. He's a man on a mission."

Laura, clearly intrigued, turned to Will. "What do you mean?"

"He has a theory that the ocean is evaporating because the earth is hot . . . and he's proven this to himself by putting a bowl of water out in the sun on a hot day, when eventually half of it evaporated. So, he concluded the same thing must be happening gradually to the ocean on a grand scale."

"That sounds rather wacky."

"Wait until I tell you the rest of it. He took this same half-empty bowl of water and dropped a bunch of pebbles in it until the water rose to the brim. Based on that, he concluded that by dropping a rock into the ocean every day, it would prevent the sea level from dropping too low; and that if other people did it, we could save the world from vanishing oceans."

"Wow, sounds like a crazy man to me!" Laura swatted a fly that was hovering too close to her half-empty can of soda. It masterfully eluded her and made a quick loop around, only to retreat again as her hand swung back reflexively.

Will added, "Well, that's Mr. Fogarty's hypothesis, and that's what gets him out of bed every day. He also believes we might even get lucky when a ship sinks, because that's worth several thousand pebbles."

"Good grief!" Laura exclaimed. "That man is a certified nut! I love the way he thinks, though—so brilliant yet so illogical! But what made him decide that the world was getting warmer in the first place?"

"The *Farmers' Almanac.*"

"Hmm . . . he really did his homework then . . ." The fly came back and briefly touched down on top of Laura's soda can. She immediately waved it away, wiped off the rim and gulped down what remained of her drink. Then she reached in her bag and pulled out a tube of sunscreen, applying it to her face, arms and legs. It was about three o'clock in the afternoon, and the sun's rays easily penetrated beyond the edges of the beach umbrella, which seemed a lot smaller now than when they'd loaded up their car earlier in the day.

"Here, put some on," she said, handing Will the sunscreen.

"I don't need it," he rejoined with a wry smile.

She sighed heavily and made a face, before tossing the sunscreen back into the bag. "I think you like doing that just to aggravate me."

"Maybe so."

They sat in a calm, relaxed silence for a while, until Will remarked, "I can't believe you never went to the beach as a child. I thought every kid around here spent all their summers there."

Laura looked thoughtful, her blue eyes trained on the distance. "It does seem a bit weird when I look back on it, but it didn't seem strange at the time. My mom felt the beach was too dangerous, with the risk of drowning, sharks, jellyfish and skin cancer, not to mention the inconvenience caused by getting sand in your shoes and clothes."

"Had she ever been?" Will asked.

"That's the interesting thing—she's never been. All her knowledge was based on what she'd seen on the news or heard other people say, but that was enough for her."

"She just doesn't seem like that kind of person—I'd never have guessed that, knowing what I know of her," Will mused, shaking his head.

Laura's gaze roamed around the clusters of people in their immediate vicinity. "This place has changed quite a bit since the time we were growing up. I remember you were the first black kid I'd ever seen, and I'm sure it was the same for most of the kids in our school. That must have been tough."

"I hated it, and I hated my parents for moving here! Suffolk was a nice place, and I had lots of friends and enjoyed school. They kept saying that Virginia Beach was much nicer, and that we'd make lots of friends, but for the first few months it was horrible. After a while, things began to get better, especially after I started coming to the beach after school and on weekends. Mr. Fogarty would occasionally stop to talk to me and tell me about his plan to save the ocean. I liked him because he never seemed to notice that I was black. Even now, twenty years later, he still calls me 'kid,' just like he did the first day I saw him."

"Moving back here has brought back a lot of interesting childhood memories. I wasn't too thrilled about leaving Atlanta—I'll be the first to admit—but maybe this is all going to work out alright," Laura said hopefully.

"We'll be fine, Laura. You worry too much. I think you derive pleasure in torturing yourself, trying to figure out all the different ways things could go wrong."

Chapter One

LAURA WAS COMPLETELY unprepared for the day Will came home and announced his decision to quit his job. They'd been living in Atlanta eleven years and everything was going well. He had seemingly enjoyed his practice, and the five other doctors he worked with were warm, genuine people they both liked.

"Why?" asked Laura, feeling the disquiet start to well up inside her.

Will shrugged. "I don't know, Laura. I just don't think I can keep doing this same thing day in, day out for the rest of my life. I need a change."

"Did you just decide this today?" she asked calmly, trying to control the pace of her breathing. "I thought you were happy here."

Will kicked off his shoes and sank into the couch; then reaching for the remote, turned on the TV to the sports channel. It was clear he didn't want to pursue the conversation.

Laura sighed and started to walk away, then changed her mind and went around the couch to where the remote was and turned off the TV. "Listen here, mister," she said angrily, her voice trembling, "you are not about to walk in here and tell me you quit your job, and then decide not to talk about it anymore. Not happening!"

Will shrugged and sat upright. He wore a nonchalant expression, seeming to be a little surprised at her reaction, which only infuriated her more.

"Okay, babe, what do you want to know?"

"What do I want to know? You just quit your job with no warning, and you're asking me what I'd like to know!"

"Look, Laura, I'm tired of going to work every day and listening to people telling me their problems, and having to spend hours writing long notes no one will read just so I can get paid by the insurance companies. During my residency, we focused on dealing with only what mattered to the patient. Now, I feel like I've turned into a clerk with an MD at the end of my name, spending long hours at work and on nights and weekends just charting, charting, charting—it never ends!"

"Okay, so what are you . . . no, what are *we* going to do now? You do realize that your decision affects me—I'm your wife. It might have been helpful to let me in on what you were thinking before you made the decision." Laura's tone was somewhat calmer, though deceptively so; her face was flushed, and her tight grip on the remote made it evident that all was not well.

"I decided to take a job as medical director of an insurance company; it's a regular eight to five job with no nights and weekends," Will explained, "and it comes with the same salary I have now."

"An insurance company? Wait, aren't they the enemy? And now you're going to work for them?" Laura was clearly nonplussed.

Will smiled awkwardly and shrugged. "Well, you know what they say—if you can't beat 'em . . ."

Laura rolled her eyes. "Okay, Will, at least you have another job lined up. When do you leave your current job and start the new one?"

"I gave them three months' notice, after which it will take me another month to get settled before starting the new job, which is in Virginia Beach. So we'll need to move . . ." His words trailed off as he saw the color drain from Laura's face. The remote fell out of her hand onto the carpet. Without another word, she started heading upstairs to the bedroom.

"Hey babe, can we talk about this?"

She heard him calling out to her, but she kept on walking until she reached the bedroom and locked the door. Then she collapsed on the bed and began sobbing uncontrollably. After about half an hour, she heard him knocking on the door. "Go away!" she yelled.

"I'm sorry, babe—please open this door," he entreated.

"Get lost, buddy!"

"Can we talk?"

"There's nothing to talk about now—get lost!"

After a while, the knocking stopped and he went away. She lay there, smarting with rage, her face buried in the pillow and her fists clenched. At some point she must have fallen asleep, because when she looked around it was ten o'clock and the room was dark. She stumbled out of bed and closed the curtains, then went into the bathroom and turning on the light, looked in the mirror. She looked pitiful. Her hair was disheveled and she had smudges of mascara around her eyes, which bore a distant, worn-out expression.

♒

William Henry Young had struggled to make friends after entering Taylor Middle School as the only child of color in his class. For the first few days, he sat alone at his own table at lunchtime, distractedly toying with his food, painfully aware of the gazes directed at him, as the other students either completely ignored him or snickered over remarks they made under their breath. On his fifth day at the school, Laura left her usual place at lunch and sat across from him. He didn't even look up when she set her tray on the table.

"Hi!" she said brightly.

"Hi," he mumbled without looking up.

"You're new here?"

He nodded, but didn't take his eyes off his plate.

"I'm Laura. Welcome to Taylor," she said, reaching across the table to shake his hand.

"I'm Will." He shook her proffered hand limply.

"Where did you come from, Will?"

"Suffolk."

"Oh, my grandma used to live in Suffolk. I've been there a few times to visit her."

Will wasn't much of a talker. In fact, for the most part, their conversations consisted of Laura asking questions and Will grunting a reply, but she didn't seem to mind. After a while, though, he started to make other friends in the school and stopped coming to the table they shared. Eventually, she gave up and went back to her old table. They still ran into each other every now and then in class or in the hallways.

Will didn't have many favorable memories of that first year when his family moved to Virginia Beach. His father had been a judge in Norfolk, the preeminent city in the coastal conurbation of Hampton Roads in southeast Virginia. Norfolk was midway between rural Suffolk, where they lived, and the up-and-coming Virginia Beach. Mr. and Mrs. Young had become concerned over the years that the schools and amenities in Suffolk were somewhat limited, and they had heard that the new schools and neighborhoods in Virginia Beach were worth looking into. They were committed to giving their two sons the best possible start in life, keenly aware it was something they'd lacked, having grown up in penury as the children of sharecroppers in neighboring North Carolina. Ignoring the squawking protestations of their sons—whose primary objection was about being taken away from their friends—they made the choice any good parent would make.

Will was the older sibling—he was twelve at the time of the move, while his brother Duncan was nine. Duncan seemed to settle in effortlessly at his school, making friends on the first day. It wasn't long before he was invited over to his friends' houses on the weekends. Will, on the other hand, struggled socially. Sometimes the kids at school hurled insults at him; and once he got into a fight and was almost suspended. Both he and Duncan excelled academically and were at the top of their class. That might have been the reason Will escaped harsher punishment after the fight, although it might just as easily have been because of his father's prominent status as a judge, as well as his mother's domineering presence in the PTA.

Later on, Will attended university in Charlottesville, followed by medical school and residency training in family medicine in Atlanta, after which he joined a practice in the area. Duncan studied computer programming at a time when many people still had trouble seeing computers as anything more than giant calculators or easy-erase typewriters. He moved to California afterward and settled there, only occasionally finding his way back to Virginia when his mother voiced her displeasure at his being away too long.

Will had lost touch with Laura after middle school, and their paths didn't cross again until a chance encounter in a grocery store in Richmond. She was college student working the evening shift there, trying to make some money for living expenses. Will was attending college in Charlottesville, but he was in Richmond at the time visiting friends.

"You look very familiar," he said to her as she rang up his purchases.

"Yeah, I get that a lot," she remarked matter-of-factly with a smile. "I think I have a 'generic white girl' look." She took his credit card and glanced at it as she prepared to run it through the machine. "William H. Young . . . hmm . . . that name is familiar. Wait a second, did you grow up in Virginia Beach? Taylor Middle School?"

Will's brow furrowed. "Yes, I did, but I'm blanking on your name," he said hesitantly.

"Laura Sullivan. I'm the girl who sat with you at lunch when you were new to the school, remember? The first person ever to point out to you that your initials spell the word 'WHY'—at least that's what you told me back then."

"Oh, hey Laura, it's great to see you. It's been ages!"

A number of other customers had joined the line, so they hastily concluded their reunion, but exchanged contact information and promised to keep in touch. By the time Will was moving to

Atlanta two years later, the two talked often and visited frequently. In fact, at some point, the possibility of a future life together began to show up with some frequency in their conversations. Finally, after completing her degree in education, Laura took a teaching job at an elementary school in Atlanta to be close to Will while he was in medical school.

When they announced their intention to marry, neither of them could have anticipated the firestorm of opposition they encountered.

"Dad, I thought you'd like to know I've proposed to a girl I've been seeing," Will told his father over the phone one day.

"You what!"

"Uh . . . there's this girl I've been dating for a while, and I think it's time we got married."

There was a long pause on the other end of the line, then some muffled sounds, as his dad held his hand over the mouthpiece and whispered to someone. His mother came on the line.

"Hello, Will," she said. "What's going on?"

He repeated the news, in a somewhat less triumphant tone. Laura, who was sitting beside him, had a nervous expression on her face.

"Who's the girl?" his mother asked.

Will tried to explain who she was, but besides saying she was in his middle school and he ran into her in a grocery store a few years before, there wasn't much else he could do to give them a clearer picture.

"Alright, Will," his mother said tersely, "why don't you bring your lady friend over this weekend so we can meet her. Is that possible?"

"Er . . . okay . . . I'll bring her over this weekend."

The phone call was on Wednesday, and an agonizing wait ensued until Saturday. The eight-hour drive to Virginia Beach seemed endless, and Will and Laura maintained an anxious silence for most of the drive.

"Don't worry, Laura, it'll be just fine," he said to her as they got out of the car in the driveway and walked up towards the house.

It wasn't. Judge Young wore a taciturn expression that many a defendant in his court had seen as they waited to hear their fate. Mrs. Young's hostility was only mildly disguised, and her conversation was, to all intents and purposes, an inquisition. She had watched them come up from the car towards the house, and the "Oh, my God!" groan that her husband overheard came from her first glance at Laura and the sudden realization that her son's fiancée was white.

"So, Laura, do your parents live in Virginia Beach?"

"My mother lives in Magnolia Circle."

Mr. and Mrs. Young exchanged quick glances regarding what they had heard and not heard. Magnolia Circle was a working-class neighborhood on the other side of town, and most of the people there were decent citizens. But if your car happened to break down there after dark, the disreputable residents were the ones who came out to meet you, and their misdeeds had earned the neighborhood a less than stellar reputation. Will's parents also noted that there was no mention of a father. From there on, the staccato clinking of silverware on plates became the discordant soundtrack of the awkward, seemingly interminable encounter. After dinner, Laura, visibly uncomfortable from the encounter, excused herself and asked Will to drop her off at her mother's house, where she had planned to spend the night before the two returned to Atlanta the following day.

For the first hour of their drive back home, neither of them said a word—until Laura broke the silence. "Your mother hates me!"

"Not really, she's just a cautious person," Will replied lamely, unable to convince even himself.

"No, she hates me. I'm pretty sure of that. Your dad is a bit harder to read, so I might give him the benefit of a doubt, but there was no pretending with your mom."

Silence ensued once again as they retreated into their thoughts, lulled by the steady hum of tires rolling over asphalt. It was a Sunday afternoon, and the proximity of Monday morning added another layer of gloom to the morose atmosphere in the vehicle.

"How did your mom handle the news?" Will asked after a while.

"She doesn't really care—one way or another—as long as there's booze at the reception."

They got to Atlanta about six-thirty in the evening and Will dropped Laura off at her apartment. Whether it was the busy schedules of the week that followed or a subconscious desire on the part of both to avoid the knotty situation that beset them, the two didn't speak until the following weekend.

Will telephoned on Saturday, around midmorning. "So, did we break up or something?" he asked, half-nervous and half-joking.

"It does feel like it; but if we did, it wasn't because of me."

"Me neither."

The question of what to do about Will's parents remained; and when they had their next serious conversation on the subject four weeks later nothing had changed. Moreover, Will knew the fact that he hadn't heard from his parents at all since the visit was an ominous sign.

"We're going to have to decide what to do if they don't get on board," said Laura wearily as they sat in a restaurant, conversing in low tones. She was a bit exasperated by his somewhat offhand approach to dealing with the situation.

He looked out the window as he took a big gulp of coffee before fixing his eyes on her. "Okay, here's what we'll do. If we haven't heard from them in another month, we should go down to city hall and get married. We can always have a more elaborate ceremony later on, when we can afford it, and when the folks have come around."

"What if they don't come around?"

"I'm sure they will eventually."

"But what if they don't?"

"Well, in that case, it's their problem and not ours."

Laura took in a deep breath and sighed. This was not quite how she'd envisioned them handling it. "Okay, supposing we do it that way—would we tell them afterwards that we got married, or just pretend like nothing happened?"

Will pondered the question for a moment. "Well, I guess there are good arguments either way. On the one hand, maybe it's better to just tell them outright and they can deal with it however they want. On the other, since we live so far from them and our paths don't cross much, we could wait and then break it to them after a while."

"I don't like the idea of keeping the marriage secret, but given that your parents are paying your tuition and expenses for medical school, it might be better to hold off on telling them until you graduate," Laura suggested.

The server came by to see if they needed anything else, and they both asked for another cup of coffee.

Laura was suddenly overtaken by a thrill of nervous excitement. "Are we really going to do this?"

"I'm ready whenever you are," Will said, grinning broadly. He was pleased and relieved to see the change in Laura at the unexpected prospect of an immediate marriage.

Chapter Two

WILL TURNED ONTO a narrow, shaded side road off Little Neck Road that was lined with crape myrtles, their exuberant coral blooms arrayed in a vivid explosion of color. Slowing down, he searched for the address of the office complex he was looking for on the left-hand side of the road.

"Eleven ninety-seven . . . there it is," he mumbled to himself as he spotted it, turning onto a winding 200-yard driveway bordered by dense shrubbery that led to a spacious parking lot. It was adjacent to a five-story office complex with a tan exterior and dark-green windows.

It was about eleven o'clock in the morning. After parking his car, he headed over to the main entrance and approached the security desk.

"May I help you, sir?" said the uniformed guard, who appeared to be in his twenties.

"I'm looking for Iatros Solutions."

"Sure, but first I'll need to see some ID, and you'll need to sign in here. Then you can take the elevators to the third floor. Their office is right across the hallway from the elevator."

Will pulled out his driver's license from his wallet and showed it to the man, then signed in and continued as directed. Once he stepped outside the elevator, he went over to a set of glass doors emblazoned with an artfully designed logo that read IATROS in a calligraphic font. As he entered, he saw the reception desk to his left, where a well-dressed woman smiled at him.

"Good morning, sir, how may I help you?"

"My name is Dr. Young. I'm a new hire here, reporting for my orientation session."

"Oh, yes—Tina is expecting you. I'll let her know you're here. Please have a seat."

Tina appeared five minutes later and asked him to follow her. She was about five foot four, probably in her early fifties, with a charming, effervescent manner.

"Hello Dr. Young, it's very nice to meet you!" she said enthusiastically. "I hope you didn't have any trouble finding us." Her voice was husky and confident, with an unmistakable New York accent.

"I had no trouble at all," Will said reassuringly.

"Come this way and I'll introduce you to the rest of the staff," Tina said.

Will followed her as she headed down a brightly lit hallway, and then turned right into a somewhat cramped room partitioned into about eight cubicles—six were rather small and two were somewhat larger.

"Everyone, I'd like you to meet our new medical director, Dr. Young," Tina announced.

There was the sound of movement with chairs being pushed back, then smiling faces emerged from the cubicles one by one, as their occupants approached him with outstretched hands.

"This is Audrey . . . that's George . . . Aisha . . . and that's Tracey . . . where's Phil?"

"He's on a phone call. He'll be out shortly," said Audrey.

"So, this is our team, our claims reviewers, who are usually the first point of contact," Tina explained. "If a claim doesn't match up with one of the approved procedure codes, or is outside the guidelines—like a colonoscopy request sooner than is usually recommended, or a mammogram is ordered for someone under forty—the computer will flag the request and bring it to their attention.

"Their job is to review the doctor's note to see if there's an obvious explanation as to why it's needed—for example, a thirty-five-year-old woman getting a mammogram, which is generally too young, but the doctor has indicated she has a lump or a strong family history of breast cancer. In that case, they can override the system and approve the request. If the explanation is still not clear, they can request additional info and then kick it up to me—the nurse—for review.

"Their training is in medical billing and coding, so they don't have a medical background—only you and I do. If I review a claim and I'm not able to make a determination, then I'll send it through to you. And as the medical director, you can either make a decision based on your review of the information, or you can speak with the doctor who ordered the test or treatment to confirm that it's appropriate."

Will nodded his understanding.

"Welcome, Dr. Young, we're happy to have you here," Tracey said, as her colleagues echoed their agreement.

Just then, Phil emerged from his cubicle and ambled over to them. He was an overweight man in his mid-fifties with an unruly red beard. He had more hair on his face than his head, since he was starting to go bald.

"Oh, hello, is this our new medical director? I'm sorry I missed the introductions. My name is Phil," he said with an arm outstretched in Will's direction.

The two shook hands enthusiastically.

"So, Dr. Young, to whose loss do we owe our good fortune?" he asked.

"I beg your pardon?"

"Where were you working before joining Iatros?"

"I was working at a practice in Atlanta for about four years, until I reached the point where I felt I needed something different."

"Is this your first time in Virginia Beach?" ventured Audrey.

"No, actually, I grew up around here, then left for college and haven't been back since."

"Alright guys," Tina interjected politely, "there'll be plenty of time for socializing later. Let me show our doctor where the break room is and finish the rest of the tour so I can get him over to the IT folks in time for his computer training—which I believe is scheduled to start in about fifteen minutes."

Will and Tina continued on, as the others returned to their desks.

"Iatros is the biggest healthcare management company in the country," Tina explained. "We're not an insurance company—but people confuse us for one all the time. What we do is help insurance companies do their job better by weeding out bogus claims, or unnecessary tests and procedures. Our little pod, with the folks you just met, manages Virginia, West Virginia, DC, Maryland, Delaware, Pennsylvania and Ohio. There's another group in this office that manages North Carolina and five other states in the region. Our headquarters is in Atlanta—and if I'm not mistaken—our company has a presence in every state east of Texas. There's a few other companies like us in Illinois, California and Oregon, but we are by far the biggest."

Tina was fast and efficient, and as she walked briskly through the office knocking on doors and making brief yet invariably pleasant introductions, she continued to regale him with impressive facts about the company she clearly believed in.

"So, that's the layout of the office. We own this floor and the two above. IT is on the next floor, which is where I'm going to take you. The corporate folks are on the top floor. After your training with IT, I believe you'll be done for the day, at least according to the itinerary emailed to me."

As they took the elevator to the next floor, Will debated whether or not to ask a question, and then decided to go ahead with it. "Do you like this place?"

She looked at him somewhat quizzically, as the merest trace of a smile formed on her lips, while the erstwhile focused, intense expression on her face softened slightly. "It meets my needs."

"Oh, I see," he replied hesitantly, not quite sure what she meant.

As the elevator doors opened and she escorted him to the IT department, she had a parting comment. "One thing I always tell people, Will, is that if you don't know what you're looking for, you may not know when you find it. I've seen many people drift from one job to another and never seem happy. In many cases it's simply because they don't know what they're looking for. So try to figure out what your needs are, if you haven't already. Then you'll be able to determine if they're being met or not."

Chapter Three

AFTER THEY RETURNED to Virginia Beach, the first six months went the way Laura feared they would. Will was excited about his job for about a month, then the complaining she'd grown accustomed to in Atlanta started up again. She'd learned over the years she could get away with an intermittent "Hmm" or "Uh-huh" whenever he maundered through his litany of woes, not needing to pay close attention to everything he was saying. In any case, he never paused to ask her opinion, so she didn't have to worry about being caught unawares by a question. She did wonder, though, whether she'd thereby missed significant clues about his desire to leave his previous job in the months prior to his unexpected and distressing announcement.

It wasn't long before she found a job as a third-grade teacher at a school in Norfolk, which was a thirty-minute drive from their house. It was in an economically disadvantaged part of town, so she immediately connected with some of the challenges her students faced, such as coming to school hungry because the fridge was empty, or not having a parent to help them with their homework because the only one available—usually the mother—was either working, exhausted, unable to help or passed-out drunk. While she'd been lucky enough to attend good schools in her childhood, it wasn't because her family was better off than any of the children she taught. It was merely an accident of geography. The line that had separated her school district from the neighboring one—which was very similar to where she was currently teaching—had been advantageously located in relation to her childhood home. She never really felt a sense of belonging with the kids she went to school with, but she'd learned to fit in inconspicuously.

Laura remembered the time her friend Leslie Watson had invited her to her house for a playdate at the age of eight. Her mother normally declined these invitations without much thought, but this once had said yes, probably because she'd said no so many times before, and didn't have the energy to go through with the tearful, sulking remonstrations that usually followed. On the appointed Saturday, Laura hopped into her mother's beat-up, dented maroon Ford Escort and they drove to Leslie's house, a dense cloud of fumes trailing the faithful jalopy like a comet tail.

"Wow, that place looks like a mansion!" her mother exclaimed as she spotted it, and then double-checked the address she'd written down on a piece of paper.

As they walked up the driveway, Leslie came running out of the house, followed by her mother whose eyes cast intermittent perplexed glances at the decrepit automobile.

"I'm glad to meet you," Mrs. Watson said to her mother with a tight, forced smile. "Leslie talks about Laura all the time. I'm glad she could come."

Laura's mother chatted with her briefly, seemingly

unperturbed by her counterpart's discomfiture, and then turned to leave.

"I'm happy to bring her back to your house at five, if you like," Mrs. Watson offered.

"No thanks," Laura's mother replied. "I'll be in the area around that time, so it shouldn't be a problem to stop back and pick her up."

That evening, there was the inevitable review of the day's visit.

"Leslie's house is huge, and she has her own bathroom in her bedroom. I had so much fun there!" Laura told her gleefully.

Her mother smiled but remained silent.

"Mom, are we poor?"

There was a mirthless chuckle from her mother. "I don't make much money, sweetie, but we get by."

"Do you think Leslie can come and visit me here?"

"Aw, I don't know," Laura's mother said, wincing. "There's not much room to play around here, and we have a lot of stuff going on. But maybe in a few weeks' time if she wants to come. We can think about it."

But Leslie never did express a desire to come and visit. In

fact, the Monday after their weekend playdate, she was somewhat distant and didn't seem to want to be in Laura's company. This was puzzling, because up until the moment Laura left, she kept saying how it was the best playdate she'd ever had. "You're my best friend, Laura!" Leslie said when her mother came upstairs to let them know Laura's mother had arrived.

After a few days of awkward interactions, Laura had rightly concluded that she and Leslie were no longer friends, and she had moved on. Now, years later, as Laura dealt with her students and tried to read behind the blank stares, sleepy faces, crumpled clothes and recurrent excuses for incomplete homework, she realized that these were her people. The people from Eldridge Elementary and Taylor Middle and High schools were not her people and had never been; she'd grown up a pretender in their midst, always uncomfortable about who she was and struggling to fit in.

She and Will had bought a house at Fisherman's Point, a 4,000-square-foot home in a quiet area, with polite neighbors who always seemed to be probing behind their casual questions. In some ways, these encounters reminded her of her schooldays. The conversations became even more tortured when she was with Will, and many times the shadow of what was not being said eclipsed what actually was.

If it had been up to her, she would've preferred living in a town house in a less ostentatious neighborhood, like the one they had in Atlanta. But Will was fixated on the offerings the realtor had lined up for them, after artfully extracting information regarding his profession.

"I don't know, Will, I think this house is too big for us. There's only the two of us right now," she protested after he brought her back to one of the houses they'd viewed earlier in the day.

"But babe, it's a great neighborhood, and a nice quiet place to relax when you're away from work. Don't you want that?"

"Sure I do, but we could find that in a smaller house. We just haven't looked."

Will pursued the property in Fisherman's Point, enraptured by the vision he had of the two of them living happily there, and taking walks or riding bikes over the weekend. At some point, Laura gave up and decided it was a fight not worth having.

Their relationship puttered along with a level of dysfunction that was more or less average for most marriages, as far as she could tell. But there were a couple of issues that steadily gnawed away at her peace of mind.

She was pushing her shopping cart out of the grocery store one Saturday when she heard a loud excited voice calling out to her.

"Laura, is that you!"

She saw a smiling lady with sunglasses who'd been walking past her, pause and turn towards her. The face looked vaguely familiar, but it wasn't until the sunglasses came off that a name and context surfaced from the recesses of Laura's memory.

"Do you remember me now?"

"Wait . . . Debbie . . . I'm trying to remember your last name—was it Shaughnessy?"

"It was. I'm Debbie Milton now."

A conversation ensued as they chatted excitedly about the years that had passed since Taylor Middle School.

"You'll never guess who I ran into the other day," Debbie said. "Will Young! He moved back into town recently, and he told me he's in touch with you."

Debbie didn't notice Laura's expression souring, and kept on prattling inanely, until Laura excused herself and walked hastily to her car. "In touch!" she repeated disbelievingly, as she sat in her car trembling with rage and fighting back tears. "I've been married to him for nine years, and he says we're in touch!"

When she brought up the subject with Will that evening, he was merely dismissive.

"Laura, you know Debbie's not the brightest person around, and she just keeps rambling on and on. I was simply trying to extricate myself from the conversation as quickly as I could. If I told her we were married, she would've kept me there talking to her for another hour."

"How about your parents then?" Laura said flatly.

Will looked at her, puzzled. "What about my parents?"

"We've been married nine years and you still haven't told them we're married. When we moved here you said you'd talk to them, but you haven't. I overheard you when you called your mom to tell her you'd moved back here. There was absolutely no mention of me."

Will let out a heavy sigh and shook his head. "Laura, you know how it is with my parents. We have to break it to them slowly."

"Nine years, Will. How, much more time do they need?"

"C'mon, babe . . ."

"Is it because you're ashamed of me?"

"Of course not!" he protested.

"Will, this isn't normal, and it bothers me a lot. If you'd like, I can call your mother and just tell it like it is, so you don't have to agonize about how and when to do it," she offered blithely, but her tone made it sound like a threat.

"No, let me do it. You know, babe, I'm just trying to protect you."

Laura let out a shrill sarcastic laugh, which surprised her as much as it did him. "I'm honored you would go to such lengths to protect me, but I think I'm ready to face whatever comes with telling them about us, so you better tell them soon. Otherwise, I'll have to do it myself."

Chapter Four

WHEN WILL LOGGED into his work computer on the first day of work, he realized that his job might be quite a bit more complicated than he'd assumed. There were seventy-seven messages waiting in his email queue, about ten of which had been flagged as high-priority with a red exclamation mark. Since Tina's cubicle was directly across from his, he asked her about them.

"I have a bunch of messages in my inbox, and I'm trying to figure out which ones I should work on and which ones have already been dealt with."

"Let me take a look," she said, coming over from where she sat, and peering at his screen through her bifocals. She scrolled through them, mumbling to herself, and then straightened up after she got to the bottom of the page. "These are all new," she said confidently. "Dr. Walker cleaned out her messages before she left, and these have all come in over the past week."

Will let out a soft involuntary groan, and he thought he might have heard a soft snicker from George's cubicle, though it could easily have been a sneeze.

"Anything else I can help you with?" Tina asked, with an aloof smile.

"Thanks, and no—that's it," he replied.

He clicked on the first message, which read "Request for abdominal MRI by Dr. Wilson, Roanoke, VA for possible GIST liver metastases in patient with neurofibromatosis; MD says CT scan will be inadequate and would like to skip directly to MRI. Please approve or schedule call with ordering MD."

He reviewed his options. He could either do some more research on what sounded like a complex, nuanced issue, or he could arrange a phone call with the requesting physician. Alternatively, he could save himself some time and click on the green box for "Approve" and move to the next one. There was always the fourth option of saying no to something he knew nothing about. He clicked on the green box.

Next item: "Request for approval of imatinib by Dr. Patel, Charleston WV for treatment of dermatofibrosarcoma protuberans . . ."

"Dermato—what!" he muttered under his breath disbelievingly, the expression on his face now a tight grimace, while he silently moved his lips as he tried to pronounce the word. Was that even a real diagnosis?

Charleston sounded like a big city, where specialists might congregate. One of his college roommates was from Charleston, though he couldn't remember if it was the one in South Carolina or the one in West Virginia. Pondering the question for a few seconds, he determined that regardless of whether it was in South Carolina or

West Virginia, Charleston was probably a big enough city to attract a doctor with expertise in treating that dermatofibro-whatever condition, and that physician probably knew what they were doing. Again, he clicked on "Approve."

Next item: "Request for approval of spine MRI in forty-five-year-old patient with low back pain. Ordering physician Dr. Cunningham, Mansfield OH."

Will's heart raced with excitement—finally something familiar! He clicked on the link to see the notes the doctor's office had sent, but the information was sketchy. He knew the guidelines governing MRI requests, so this was worth a conversation with the doctor. He noted that the ordering doctor was a family practitioner, which made it less likely that he would know something Will didn't know. He requested a phone call with the ordering doctor. He was making progress.

Next item: "Request for approval of MRA/MRV in fifty-six-year-old female with headache, concern for dural venous sinus thrombosis. Requesting physician Dr. Kenilworth, Pittsburgh, PA."

He gritted his teeth. Dural venous sinus thrombosis was not a condition he'd ever directly managed, but he knew enough about it from medical school to know it was not usually a benign affliction. Still, he needed more information. He paused for a second, then his face lit up. Clicking on the Internet browser icon on his computer, he searched for Dr. Kenilworth. A picture of a stern bespectacled female in her late fifties appeared. She was the head of neurosurgery at the University of Pittsburgh, with an intimidating array of titles underneath her name. He clicked on the green box.

He was gradually developing a rhythm. Most of the requests sounded reasonable; and even when there were questions, it seemed like a phone call with the ordering physician would resolve the issue.

Tina's voice broke into his thoughts. "Oh, by the way, Dr. Young, is the link for the specialty guidelines working? Dr. Walker said she was having trouble with it before she left."

"Er . . . what link?" he asked, looking puzzled.

"Here, let me show you," she said, getting up from her desk and coming over to his. She minimized his other windows and clicked on an icon labeled "Guidelines." It wasn't working.

"Looks like we'll need the IT folks to take a look at this ASAP, otherwise it'll make your work much more difficult. There are so many specialty guidelines that it would be impossible to keep up with all that information without using the "Guidelines" link. It's easily searchable and a great time-saver—much easier than trying to research every question out on the Internet." Tina paused as she studied Will's screen. "Wow! It looks like you're already making lots of progress, even without the link!" she remarked. Then she maximized the windows she'd minimized and returned to her desk.

He nodded, while cursing her inwardly. Surely, they didn't

expect him to research every question that came through—or did they? That would take an insanely huge amount of time. He looked to see how many messages he'd tackled—there were twelve. He clicked on the refresh icon at the top of the page, to purge them from the queue. When the screen refreshed, there were eighty-one messages remaining. An additional sixteen messages had come in! His jaw tensed up and he frowned at the screen, resisting a strong desire to punch it. Instead, he got up and headed over to the break room, poured himself some coffee, and stood by the window. He looked out over the parking lot towards the elegant multistoried houses that poked through the dense green cover of trees in the distance. When he was growing up, the area had been all wild forest with only an occasional farmhouse here and there.

"This is a well-hidden place. Most people don't even know that it exists." A voice roused Will from his introspection.

It was George, a tall, slender individual in his fifties, with dark hair that had been dyed to suppress any hints of aging, and a short, well-groomed beard. He wore small, round rimless glasses. He came in armed with his favorite maroon mug and a tea bag, and proceeded to fill up the mug from the hot water dispenser. He always carried his own tea bags wherever he went, having been known to pull one out of his pocket at a restaurant or party on more than one occasion. It was invariably the same brand of green tea.

Will had heard about the time George left his beloved mug behind in the break room, when a newbie made the grave error of using it for her coffee. When he found his unwashed mug sitting in the sink contaminated by coffee sediment, he flew into a rage. Had it not been for Tina's timely intervention, things might have turned out much worse than they did. Even after the culprit scrubbed the mug clean and apologized numerous times for her error, George had carried it home with him that evening in a plastic bag, ostensibly to sterilize it. For him, that afternoon had been a long one, since he'd had to do without his customary tea break. There was no chance he'd use one of the Styrofoam cups that were stacked up on the countertop, acutely conscious as he was of their destructive impact on the environment. The unfortunate newbie had lasted about a week before she requested a transfer to a different department.

After George had filled up his mug with steaming hot water, he slowly submerged his tea bag and carefully draped its string over the side. He came and stood by the window next to Will.

"So, how are you liking it so far?" he asked cheerfully.

Will shrugged. "I'm not sure yet. I'm still trying to figure it out."

"I bet it feels a whole lot different from taking care of patients. Dr. Heidi used to complain all the time about having to keep up with all the literature and guidelines for the different specialties, while having to decide on the merits of a claim in the limited amount of time available."

"Who's Dr. Heidi? Is she the doctor who was here before

me?" Will asked.

"Yes. She kept telling us to call her Heidi, rather than Dr. Walker. But I just couldn't get comfortable with that degree of familiarity, so I settled on Dr. Heidi—which she actually liked. She said it had a distinctive southern ring to it. I wouldn't know—I've lived here all my life, so I wouldn't know any different. She was one of the nicest people I've ever met. But after about three years, this place started wearing her down; and she'd gotten to the point where she would suddenly snap at you out of the blue—which was totally unlike her. She got pretty jaded towards the end. We were sad to see her go, but we were all pleased for her sake, because she was clearly unhappy here."

"Where'd she go?"

"Back to Minnesota, back to her old practice. She'd initially thought the eight-to-five schedule at Iatros would be just what she needed for her family—she had young kids and had recently been through an acrimonious divorce. She used to tell us that before she moved to Virginia Beach, she fantasized about how she and her kids would spend their weekends and evenings on the beach, especially since she'd bought a beautiful home right by the water. But things didn't quite work out that way, and she found herself working too many long days to pay for a house that was empty most of the time. And even when she was home, there seemed to be a never-ending to-do list consuming the little bit of leisure left to her."

Will listened quietly, then glanced down at his coffee cup. It was almost empty. "Well, I guess it's time to get back to work," he announced perfunctorily, gulping down what was left before tossing his cup into the trash can.

"Yup, time to hop back onto the hamster wheel. Don't let them work you too hard, Doc!" George said cheerily as he followed Will back into the office.

♒

After a little more than half a year at Iatros, Will had settled into a routine characterized by pervasive monotony. Mondays had even reclaimed that familiar depressing quality he remembered from his old practice. He tried to hide his growing sense of ennui from Laura, wanting to avoid one of those heated discussions that generally never produced a victor on either side. She at least had settled in well, and was enjoying her job.

The people he worked with were an interesting bunch, which to some extent made up for the daily drudgery. Phil, for example, was a retired navy pilot who'd visited at least half the countries in the world and set foot on every continent except Antarctica. He spent his weekends working on his hot rods, heading out every week or two to a popular racetrack in North Carolina. Starting on the Wednesday before a weekend at the races, his level of energy and excitement permeated the entire office, as if he was doing it for all of them. Audrey and Aisha had once driven out to the track to watch him compete, and the experience itself proved to be anticlimactic—although they pretended otherwise. After that, they came up with excuses when he invited them to another race.

Aisha had also been in the navy, although unlike Phil who'd retired with twenty years under his belt, she'd served only five. She was slender and athletic, with a clean-shaven head, and had a penchant for gold hoop earrings that complemented her walnut-brown skin. A compulsive jogger, she ran about seven miles every day, often more on weekends. She'd admitted to having worn out two jogging strollers since she used to bring along her infant sons—now aged nine and six—on her morning runs in earlier years. Will wondered whether she removed her earrings before she went out running, but never thought to ask.

She and Audrey got along well. Both were in their late twenties, the youngest members of the office staff. Will—about six years older—was the next above them in age. Audrey was an extremely shy and mild-mannered redhead who lived in fear of inadvertently offending someone by saying the wrong thing, the net result being that she often found herself apologizing to a bemused interlocutor for a nonexistent faux-pas. But once she became comfortable with someone, her fear vanished; her animated break-room conversations with Aisha, punctuated by screeching laughter, were strong evidence of this.

Tracey was probably in her late thirties or early forties. She had a warm, effusive personality, and was extremely scatterbrained—

perpetually searching for misplaced documents, and often missing deadlines and meetings she'd forgotten to put on her calendar. Half of the groans of disapproval emanating from George's cubicle had something to do with Tracey, although they always seemed congenial when face to face.

Tina was the matriarch of the office. She'd been there the longest and seemed to have an intuitive sense of how the company was supposed to work, often coming up with creative solutions when a situation arose for which there was neither protocol nor precedent. So naturally she was the one Will turned to when he received a message informing him of a meeting he was expected to attend with Rebecca Mancini, the company's vice president.

"Oh, don't worry about it, Doc," Tina said dismissively. "That's just the routine meeting for our physicians that occurs every six to twelve months to make sure everything is going as it should. You won't get fired or anything like that—although I will say that some docs who worked here previously said they'd prefer a root canal appointment instead."

The vice president's office was on the fifth floor, near the end of the hallway. Her secretary was on the phone, but he was clearly expected since she immediately waved him through—pointing at the half-open door and mouthing the words "go ahead" with an emphatic nod. He gave the door two light taps to signal his presence before he went inside.

Ms. Mancini was a small woman in her early sixties who wore an exorbitant amount of makeup. She had emerald green eyes and an intense gaze, which for Will evoked the image of a bird of prey.

"Good morning, Dr. Young," she said, gesturing for him to sit down. "How is everything coming along so far?"

"Everything seems fine, as far as I can tell," Will replied.

A brief, casual discourse accompanied by the usual pleasantries ensued before she disclosed the real reason for his visit.

"Tell me, Will, how would you describe your role as physician manager at Iatros?" she asked.

"Uh . . . my role is to verify the medical appropriateness of and necessity for tests and non-formulary prescriptions ordered, to ensure that optimal care is provided in a cost-efficient manner," he said, somewhat hesitantly, averting his eyes from her steely glare.

"What's the inherent assumption in that?"

He looked up, mystified, and shook his head as if he didn't understand the question.

"All the decisions we make are founded on an inherent assumption. And it's usually helpful to identify your assumptions up front in order to help you determine whether or not your decisions are based on a valid premise."

Will looked at her blankly, still not comprehending her

meaning.

"Let me help you out, Dr. Young, because I'm sure you know the answer intuitively, although you may never have verbalized it. The assumption inherent in the task is that not all tests or non-formulary prescriptions are appropriate. This may sound obvious, but over the years I've learnt that what might be obvious to me may not be obvious to you, and vice versa, because we come at this from different backgrounds. Unless we put our assumptions on the table, we may find ourselves talking at cross-purposes, all the while assuming we're talking about the same thing."

At this point, Will was somewhere between fascinated and confused.

"If all the tests and prescriptions were appropriate, would there need to be a physician manager?"

The title "physician manager," which he'd only heard for the first time from her lips, had a less dignified ring to it than "medical director," which was his official designation. Still, all he did was shake his head no in response to her question.

"What's the problem with unnecessary tests or prescriptions?"

"They drive up costs," he answered flatly.

"So, in a perfect situation—and I know we're not in a perfect situation," she added, "the dollars we pay you would come from the cost reduction by saving on unnecessary, low-value tests or inappropriate prescriptions. I think many physicians struggle to define value. It happens quite often that a doctor orders expensive tests mostly to satisfy their own curiosity, while they don't necessarily benefit the patient's health and well-being. What you have to do for this job is take off the doctor hat and put on the physician manager hat for the greater good, with your goal being to improve the overall efficiency of the system."

Ms. Mancini leaned back slightly in her black leather chair, with her hands still clasped in front of her on the glass tabletop. A cloud must have blocked the sun at precisely this moment, since the sunlight that had previously filtered through the blinds disappeared and the room darkened. Will's throat was dry, and he realized his palms were sweaty.

"Dr. Young," she said after a seemingly interminable pause, "imagine you were sitting in my chair and I came to you as a saleswoman who told you about a brilliant invention that was guaranteed to cut your monthly costs by twenty percent. In fact, I was so sure the invention would work that I was willing to rent it to you on a trial basis at a discounted rate for six months, after which you could choose to buy it. Suppose I came back to you after six months, and you reviewed your records and found that your costs had remained exactly the same, and the machine was going to cost you, say, ten thousand dollars a month for two years to purchase. Would you buy the machine, based on the results of the trial period?"

She spoke in a soft monotone, and there was no warmth in the expression on her face.

"Probably not." When he answered her question, it was clear to him he was the machine she was talking about.

"Very well, Dr. Young, I'll let you get back to your work. Please remember, we wouldn't need to hire a physician manager if we didn't believe there was a problem with low-value tests or unnecessary prescriptions. Believe me, they are out there—you just need to look for them and they'll become apparent."

As Will left her office and went towards the elevator, he felt a growing sense of trepidation as he realized the full thrust of her message. His value to the company was directly tied to the number of requests he denied. From their standpoint, the notion that most or all of the requests were medically appropriate was not financially tenable.

Chapter Five

EVEN AFTER THE conversation with Ms. Mancini, it was difficult for Will to sort through the myriad requests and determine what qualified as a low-value test and what didn't. Every case seemed to have a wrinkle that made it deviate from the average, so that he second-guessed himself every time he clicked on the red box to deny a request. Still, he found himself a bit more comfortable clicking on it, and the new pattern started showing up on his monthly report.

His usual monthly report was replete with cryptic content, including diagnostic codes and dollar values that meant nothing to him. At the bottom right-hand corner, there were two boxes with a percentage underneath. In the box on the left there was a letter "A," and in the box on the right was a letter "D." In his first few months at the job, his reports had numbers ranging from ninety to ninety-five percent underneath box A, and numbers between five and ten percent underneath box D. The number underneath box D was usually in red. About four months after his meeting with Ms. Mancini, he was reviewing his report—which at this point still didn't make much sense to him—when he noticed that the percentages in the D box had gradually increased, first to fifteen, then twenty percent, he recalled, until this one where it was thirty-three. And unlike the earlier reports where the number appeared in red, this time it was black. As the numbers under the D box increased, those in the A box decreased, so added together they always made a hundred percent. He noticed something else that was different that made his heart skip a beat. Another entry had appeared just below boxes A and D labeled "Performance Incentive." Directly across from that heading was an entry of $5,350.

"Tina, I have some questions about my current monthly report. Who can I ask?"

"Lloyd in accounts would be the best person," she said without looking up from her desk. "He's on the fifth floor, in the opposite direction from Mancini and the other bigwigs. He's very laid-back and good at explaining things."

He thanked her and checked the time on his screen. It was a good time to take a break. He printed out a copy of his report, rose from his desk and headed out to the elevator.

Lloyd had a jet-black complexion and brilliant white teeth, although a gap showed between the upper middle two when he smiled. He spoke in a soft voice with a slight Caribbean accent.

"I've been expecting you," he said with a chuckle, when Will introduced himself.

"Why?" Will was puzzled.

Lloyd elaborated. "I usually have docs coming up here for an explanation of their reports the minute they crack the sound barrier, which you just did. Up until that point, the report is meaningless numbers, just like a lottery ticket that doesn't match the jackpot. As soon as it appears you've reached some kind of threshold where there's more money coming to you, then people get curious. That's when I get a call or someone comes up here asking me to explain the numbers."

"So, what do the numbers mean?"

"Exactly what you think they mean, Dr. Young. Once you get above thirty percent denials, you receive a performance incentive—or bonus. Below thirty percent, the numbers in your D—for denials—box are red, meaning that you're not doing your job. Your goal is to try to keep your denials in the black as much as you can, though it's not always possible. The $5,350 is your bonus for being in the black last month. When and if you get a higher percentage in the denials box, your bonus will go up."

Will felt a warm surge of excitement. "Thanks for explaining it to me."

"One thing though, Doc," Lloyd said as Will turned to leave. "Beyond a certain point you'll be endangering the patients' care, so you have to carefully consider both sides. They put doctors in the position you're in because they assume you'll make the right decision and not just focus on putting more money in your pocket. I hear there's an oath you guys take to always do what's right for the patient."

"The Hippocratic oath," Will replied.

"Oh, is that how you say it?" asked Lloyd, grinning broadly. "I've always thought it was called the 'hypocritic' oath, which sounds like the opposite of what you're supposed to do."

Will smiled. "Thanks again for your help, Lloyd," he said, before leaving his office.

♒

The Iatros summer picnic was on a muggy Saturday afternoon at Mount Trashmore Park, a scenic park with gentle, rolling green hills bordering a man-made lake. It was situated on a site that had previously been an abandoned landfill, presumably the origin of the witty moniker. When the weather was nice, the park teemed with picnickers, walkers, bikers, skateboarders—and little children rolling playfully down the slopes and sprinting breathlessly back up to the top for as long as their legs could carry them.

Will arrived there at about two in the afternoon, and as he pulled into the parking lot, he spotted a few familiar figures—Tina, Aisha, Audrey and Phil—among the fifty or so attendees who were gathered under the two picnic shelters reserved for the occasion. As he walked along the footpath to join the others, he heard a car honking and a voice calling out to him. When he turned towards the sounds, his gaze fell on a gleaming, burgundy Jaguar convertible that had slowed down a short distance away from him.

"Hey, Dr. Young!" the driver called out again.

He hesitated for a moment, unsure of who it was, until the driver took off his sunglasses and he recognized George.

"Oh, hello George, I almost didn't recognize you," he rejoined, approaching the car.

"Jeff, this is Dr. Young, our medical director. Dr. Young, I'd like you to meet my cousin, Jeff."

"I've heard a lot about you, Doc," said Jeff, smiling, as he shook Will's hand. "George was bummed when Dr. Heidi left, but he says you're an adequate replacement. No one can ever quite replace Dr. Heidi in George's mind—in fact, he used to call her Wonder Woman."

Will grinned. "That's a really nice ride you got there, George!" he observed, stepping back to inspect the magnificent automobile.

"Thanks, Doc," George replied, his eyes beaming with pride. "We'll go find a parking spot, and catch up with you later."

Will continued on, but not without turning around first to get one more glimpse of the car. His whole body tingled with excitement as he followed the graceful contours of the car gliding noiselessly away from him. As he approached the picnic shed, he must have retained that dazed and dreamy expression, because Tina noticed it immediately.

"Dr. Young, you look like you just had a chance encounter with a very beautiful woman," she remarked.

Will smiled and shook his head.

"I think he's been ogling George's new car," Aisha observed matter-of-factly, while Audrey, who was sitting next to her on the picnic bench, couldn't suppress a soft giggle.

"Well, it is a really nice car!" Will exclaimed, sounding a tad defensive.

"No disrespect, Doc," Tina said with a shrug, "but I drive a pickup truck with a hundred and seventy-five thousand miles on it. The whole thing about pretty cars doesn't really work for me. I'm all about functionality."

"Tina's car is indestructible," Aisha explained. "It makes a big racket, but it's never broken down. As long as you put gas in it, it's ready to go. It's not the prettiest car in the lot, but it's reliable all right."

"Hey, I'm fifty-five with grown kids—and I live on a farm. Pretty doesn't cut it where I'm from," Tina added. "But enough about cars, let's eat!" and she started heading towards one of the tables laden with food.

Phil was manning the barbecue, while his wife Ellen, a petite gray-haired lady, shuttled back and forth, bringing the sizzling hamburgers and franks to the table nearest to where the people from Will's office were sitting. Staff from all the departments were in attendance, but everyone seemed to prefer sitting with their officemates. Aisha's husband was helping Phil, and her two children were running back and forth in the grass, blowing bubbles with little hoops they dipped into plastic jars filled with soapy water.

"Where's your family, Doc?" Aisha asked Will. "I thought you were married—or is that just bling?" pointing at his wedding band.

He flushed with embarrassment and folded his arms in front of his chest self-consciously so his ring was out of sight. "My wife couldn't come. She had some family stuff she needed to deal with," he said.

Will hadn't told Laura about the picnic, although he wasn't sure why. They interacted peaceably as long as they avoided thorny topics, such as telling his parents about their marriage. He still planned on doing it, but hadn't yet gotten around to it despite her frequent admonitions. Whenever the subject came up, her mood vacillated between anger and quiet sarcasm to stony brooding silence. She often visited her mother on weekends, either Saturday or Sunday, and spent the whole day there. And if he happened to be home when she got back in the evening, she didn't say a word about what she'd been up to. During the week, she went to bed a lot earlier than in the past—she was often asleep by eight or eight thirty. Increasingly, it seemed like they hardly spent any time together.

"How about you, Audrey, did you come alone?" he asked awkwardly.

"She's part of my family!" Aisha announced boldly, putting her arm around Audrey. "Did you know that we're almost twins? We were born a day apart."

"I didn't know that," Will admitted.

"Yup, she's October thirteenth and I'm October fourteenth. Same year."

Tina returned with some food and her husband, Carlos, whom she introduced to Will. Having been absent for most of the previous conversation, she repeated the question he'd just answered. "So, Doc, where's your wife? I was hoping we'd get to meet her today."

"She couldn't make it today, but I'll make sure she comes the next time," he said as he got up to get himself some food.

Chapter Six

WILL DETERMINED THAT neurosurgeons and oncologists were generally the specialists whose requests carried a much higher risk of things going bad in the instance of an inappropriate denial, except when a neurosurgeon's request involved back pain. So he generally gave them a wide berth and applied a much lower benchmark when clicking on the green box. Other specialties like rheumatology were more vulnerable to refusal, since there was rarely the immediate risk of death or disability. In those cases, he could afford to say no if there was no clear rationale supported by the guidelines. And usually, if the doctor felt strongly enough about their request, they'd follow up with a phone call; but a denial logged for a month still counted in his favor, even if it was reviewed and approved in the subsequent month.

He'd managed to keep his denials above thirty percent, although there were times he just barely made it. The bonuses kept rolling in: three thousand one month, five thousand the next, seven thousand . . . he found himself waiting for his monthly report with eager anticipation, and strategizing about how to meet his target for the following month.

One Friday afternoon, he was struggling to contain his excitement and restlessness. He had a big weekend ahead of him, and the minute hand of the clock seemed to be stuck in place. It was about three o'clock when Audrey's voice came over the intercom to announce he had a call. It was a certain Dr. Miller, calling to appeal Will's denial of a test he'd ordered three weeks prior. Will clicked on the link to bring up the details of the case as he picked up the phone.

"Hello, Dr. Miller—how may I assist you today?"

A somewhat gruff voice said hello and then got right to the point. "I'm calling because my patient needs a test, and I understand you're the one who denied my request."

Will's eyes quickly scanned the report as Dr. Miller spoke, re-familiarizing himself with the details. It involved a thirty-three-year-old male, Josué Pérez, who'd already undergone a sleep study that came back normal. Dr. Miller wanted to run additional tests that were more complex.

Will grimaced slightly and clenched his teeth. Lately, he'd been receiving an unusually large number of requests for sleep studies; and it seemed strange to him that this relatively rare condition had suddenly become so widespread. The tests were very expensive, as was the equipment used to treat the problem, so Will started having doubts about the veracity of so many diagnoses. In fact, sleep studies and imaging for back pain were among the staples that kept his denials column in the black.

"Hmm . . . Dr. Miller, this patient already had a sleep study that was negative . . ." Will began.

"I'm aware of that," Dr. Miller interrupted, sounding annoyed. "That's the reason I ordered the other two tests. This guy definitely has a problem and we need to figure it out, so it's quite frustrating to have to navigate all these roadblocks to get what I need for my patient."

There was something about Dr. Miller's impatience and his dismissive attitude towards Will's decision that rubbed Will the wrong way. Usually at this point, he'd be looking for a congenial way out of the impasse, particularly if it was one of those cases that could go either way. Instead, he found himself pushing back.

"But sir," he said, "I reviewed your note. The Epworth score was only ten, so that along with a negative sleep study means he doesn't meet the criteria for additional testing."

"That Epworth score is worthless!" exploded Dr. Miller. "For one thing, this guy speaks very limited English, so I'm not even sure he knew what he was answering on the questionnaire. Secondly, he was falling asleep in the exam room as I was talking to him, so who cares about the Epworth?"

Will felt the blood rushing to his face, his breathing tinged with anxiety, as he felt increasingly on the defensive. But it was what came after Miller's last remarks that rendered the situation irredeemable.

"So, what kind of doctor are you anyway?" his interlocutor asked. "Or are you a doctor?"

Will, aware that their conversation was being recorded, suppressed the urge to tell his caller it was none of his business. Instead, he exhaled deeply before he said calmly, "Is there anything else I can do for you, sir?"

"Hey, listen," Dr. Miller said, "I'm not trying to attack you—I'm just curious. In the denial letter, it stated this telephone call would be a so-called peer-to-peer conversation. Since I'm a board-certified specialist in the field of sleep medicine, I would expect that the person overriding my decision without having seen the patient would be someone with similar credentials and not, for example, a urologist or a podiatrist. You could be the smartest neurosurgeon on the planet for all I know, but that would not make you qualified to overrule my decision as a specialist . . ."

"Alright, Dr. Miller," Will interrupted, "unless you have anything else to tell me that is relevant to what I already know about this case, I'm going to hang up now."

"I'll save you the trouble, buddy," he growled, as he muttered what sounded like an expletive before the line went dead.

Will was furious and his hands were shaking. He buried his face in his sweaty palms. What a jerk! he thought.

"Is everything alright, Doc?" Tina called from across the room.

"I'm fine," he mumbled, "it was just an angry customer."

Will struggled to focus for the remainder of the afternoon, flitting half-heartedly from one task to another. There was another call that came through from George, but—claiming to be in the middle of something important—he told him to take a message, and said he'd call back first thing Monday morning.

On his way home that evening, Will drove past the Porsche dealership, casting a longing glance in its direction. He may have taken a beating that afternoon, but tomorrow was the long-awaited day that would make that stressful situation seem like a minor irritation. Since he'd first laid eyes on "Elizabeth"—which was how George fondly referred to his Jaguar—Will had been planning in earnest to buy his own dream car.

The next morning, he awoke at seven, bubbling with excitement. As he waited restlessly for Laura to wake up, he paced around the kitchen, purposely banging utensils together in a less than subtle attempt to rouse her. At about eight, she finally appeared, a bemused frown on her face.

"Good morning, princess!" he greeted her enthusiastically.

She mumbled a greeting as she retrieved her favorite coffee mug from a shelf in the cabinet, poured water and milk into it, then placed it in the microwave. When it was ready, she added two heaping teaspoons of instant coffee and sat down at the table, looking dazed and half asleep. She was not a morning person.

After she'd taken a couple of sips of coffee, she looked at

Will and said, "What's going on? Why are you up so early?"

"How would you like to go car shopping today?" he said cheerfully.

She stared at him blankly. "Why? We already have two cars that work just fine, or at least mine does. We don't need a new car."

"Well, technically that's true—we don't need a new car, but that's not the point. I want a nicer car than the one I'm driving. I've decided I need to live a little. I mean I work so hard and I'd like a better car—plus, I can afford it."

She was squinting from the brilliant sunlight coming in through the kitchen window, and Will noticed a look of irritation creeping over her face as she said angrily, "It's your money, amigo!" She rose from the table and started heading back upstairs towards the bedroom, taking her coffee with her.

"Wait, babe!" he called out to her, following her up the stairs. "Why are you getting so upset?"

She stopped at the bedroom door and turned around to face him. "I'm not upset. I just don't see how this involves me. My car's fine, and it's your money. You don't need my input, just like you didn't need it when you moved us here from Atlanta or bought this house."

"Babe, I'm sorry, I can see that you're angry . . ."

He saw a discordantly calm smile forming on her face as she said, "No, Will, I'm not angry, not anymore. Enjoy your car shopping! Maybe after you buy that fancy car you want we can drive over to your parents' house and tell them our little secret about how we've been married almost ten years. Maybe if they see us in an expensive car, things will work out better with them than they did the last time!" And with that, she stepped inside the bedroom and shut the door behind her.

Will cursed under his breath and slammed his fist into the open palm of his hand. He'd suspected she might not be as enthusiastic as he was about the new car, but he'd already made up his mind. Grabbing the car keys, he left the house and got into his car. The dealership would open at nine, which was just a few minutes away.

As he drove there, Will could feel his anger rising as he realized their relationship was nothing more than an empty shell, with periods of sterile, polite discourse punctuated by eruptions of hostility. Those days in Atlanta when they were head-over-heels in love were a distant memory. Laura had become angry and cynical, and—he couldn't help think it— somewhat stout. He was careful never to bring up the subject, but now that he thought about it, maybe he should suggest she start exercising. An image of Audrey came to his mind's eye unbidden—she had an excellent figure, toned by years of punishing workouts. And she was incapable of the kind of snarky comebacks that Laura carried in her quiver of rhetorical blow-darts.

As he entered the dealership parking lot, Will immediately spotted the car he'd decided on earlier in the week: a midnight black Porsche 911 convertible with tan leather seats and a 3.0-liter engine. A few others cars had been of passing interest to him, but with this particular vehicle it was love at first sight.

"Dr. Young," a voice called out as Will stepped into the showroom. "I see you are a man of your word, right down to the very minute you said you'd come. In my experience, there are too many people who make promises they don't intend to keep."

Mr. Randolph, the sales agent, had a penchant for flattery and hyperbole. As they seated themselves at his desk, he continued, "Are you sure that's the one you want, Dr. Young? Although I admit that every time I walk past her, I feel my heart start to flutter. She makes me want to trade mine in. Mine's an older model, but I don't want to hurt her feelings. We've been together four years now." As he spoke, he was artfully guiding Will through the financing documents with lightning speed, preventing any pauses that might allow for the interjection of any hesitation or buyer's remorse.

"So, along with your down payment of twenty-five thousand, we'll give you five thousand for your trade-in. And Doc, I'm afraid my hands are tied since the finance guy, Bill, won't let me go above that. Your old vehicle is a bit problematic for us—we'll have to call in some favors from other dealerships to see if they'd be willing to take it, because we only sell luxury cars. But I'll go ahead with the trade-in as promised as a special service to you, now that you're one of our customers. This kind of relationship is typically lifelong, so we try to do everything in our power to start things off on the right foot . . ." Randolph paused to answer Will's questions.

"Yes, that box is your monthly payment of $2,150. Sure, Doc"—fake laugh—"I know you can afford it, and you know that too . . . yup, and that's the extra coverage, which we recommend—that way if there's a mechanical fault with the car that's not covered by the warranty, you just bring it back and we'll give you a loaner while we fix it . . . uh huh . . . and down here is where you put your John Hancock, marking the first day of the rest of your life . . ."

Will was finished in no time, and he didn't waste another second away from his new car. As he sank into the soft leather seat, the intoxicating new car smell enveloped him. He turned on the engine and turned up the radio, then depressed the gas pedal just slightly, remembering the lesson he'd learned during the test drive. The car surged forward and he tapped the brake slightly, then turned left to ease it slowly out of the lot.

He knew exactly where he wanted to go on his first drive. After gliding up the ramp onto the I-264, he pressed down on the pedal and surged effortlessly into the fast-moving westbound traffic. It would take him a while to get used to the rushing wind of a convertible, particularly at higher speeds. He slowed down five minutes later to take the exit that would lead him to Mount

Trashmore Park. There were already quite a number of people in the park, and as he slowly drove past, he watched heads turn to admire his car. He tried to maintain a composed, casual demeanor, as if he was totally unaware of his vehicle's cachet and the status it automatically conferred.

After circling the park, Will turned into a quiet side road and started heading towards home. As he did, he started wondering about what Laura's reaction would be once she learned of the $120,000 price tag. Of course, she'd probably already left for her mother's house where she seemed to retreat nearly every weekend— particularly when things were not going well between them. Like last Saturday, when they'd discussed having a baby. She was ready, but he'd found the prospect of such a major disruption to their lives too daunting; so they'd shelved the topic for another day, while the tension between them remained palpable. He found himself thinking about Audrey again, and he glanced at the empty passenger seat to his side.

Suddenly, there was a flash of light on his left, and when he turned his head to find the source, he saw a grey Ford Ranger pickup truck appear out of nowhere, barreling towards him. His whole body froze in terror as a loud, high-pitched metallic crunch split the air, followed by a deafening bang. Then everything went black.

Chapter Seven

LAURA'S RELATIONSHIP WITH her mother had flourished since she and Will had settled in Virginia Beach. Years of heavy drinking had taken their toll on Ms. Sullivan, so despite being in her mid-fifties she looked at least seventy. But as Laura's weekend visits became more frequent, the bottles of rum and whisky started disappearing from the house, while her level of enthusiasm for the errands and outings her daughter planned kept on rising. Little was said about Laura's troubled marriage, because it was obvious from the beginning that her visits were in large part an attempt to escape from its miseries.

On the Saturday when Will had departed on his foolish errand, Laura felt a sense of pride as she reflected on how mature her reaction had been. As she parked her Toyota Corolla in her mother's driveway, she admitted to herself that she'd been irritated and rather more sarcastic perhaps than was dignified, but, overall, she'd expended very little emotional energy on the unpleasant exchange.

After enjoying a serene breakfast together of scrambled eggs, bacon and pancakes, the two went off to do their errands. Laura ended up doing most of her own grocery shopping at her mother's neighborhood supermarket, to the point where a couple of the regular clerks assumed she lived in Magnolia Circle. That afternoon, they visited her mother's sister, May, who lived next to a small picturesque park with a pond frequented by Canada geese. At about two o'clock, they bade farewell to Aunt May and drove back to her mother's house, where Laura had intended to drop her off and then head home. She often forgot to take her cell phone with her—leaving it at home or lying on random tabletops—a habit Will found irksome. As she saw her mother in, Laura spotted it on the kitchen table where she'd unwittingly left it.

"Oh, there's my phone!" she exclaimed, "and I didn't even know it was missing." When she picked it up, she noticed there were two calls from an hour before, from an unfamiliar number. The caller hadn't left any voicemails. "Alright, Mom. I might stop by tomorrow, depending on what's going on at home," Laura said cheerfully as she tossed the phone into her handbag and gave her mother a kiss on the cheek.

When Laura got home, she was in the process of unloading groceries from the car when she heard her cell phone ring. She put down the bags she was holding, and fumbled around for it in her handbag.

"Hello?" she answered.

"Hello, my name is Dr. Esteban, and I'm calling from Hampton Roads Medical Center. I wish to speak to Mrs. Young."

"This is she," Laura replied hesitantly, alarmed at hearing the words "medical center."

"Ma'am, I'm sorry to inform you that your husband was

involved in an auto accident earlier today. You'll need to come into the emergency department as soon as possible."

"What . . . what happened?" she heard herself say. Her voice sounded like it was coming from a long way off, and her knees were starting to get wobbly.

"Please come as soon as you can, Mrs. Young. We'll explain everything to you when you get here."

⌁

When Laura arrived at the hospital, she wandered around in a daze asking for directions to the emergency department. Once there, she approached the receptionist in the waiting area.

"My name is Laura Young. I just received a call from a Dr. Esteban that my husband was brought here earlier."

The receptionist motioned for her to take a seat in the waiting area. About seven other people were there, either alone or in pairs, sitting quietly. Most were either looking down at their phones or at the disjointed loop of news clips and scrolling messages on the TV overhead that was set to a low volume.

Laura noticed a young clean-shaven man in his twenties wearing surgical scrubs and a white coat appear at the entrance to the waiting area. He glanced around as if he were looking for someone. Apparently not finding the person he was seeking, he went up to the receptionist and whispered to her. The receptionist nodded and gestured in Laura's direction. The next thing she knew, the doctor was standing over her.

"Are you Mrs. Young?" he said.

She nodded.

"I'm Dr. Esteban—we spoke a short while ago," he said. "Please come with me."

Laura followed him into a room—the sign on the door said FAMILY CONFERENCE ROOM—and sat at a table across from him. Her heart was pounding.

"Mrs. Young, as I said on the phone, your husband was involved in a motor vehicle accident today, around eleven fifteen this morning. The police told us he was T-boned at an intersection by a truck that was moving at about fifty miles an hour. I'm sorry to say he was pretty badly hurt, and his car suffered extensive damage. From what I understand, he had just purchased the vehicle, as it still had temporary plates, and the police contacted the two dealerships in the area that sell that type of car, which is how they were able to obtain his identity and your contact information. His parents' names were on his medical records, so we got in touch with them when we couldn't initially get hold of you. They were out of town when I reached them, but they should be coming in tomorrow."

"How . . . how is . . ." she began to ask, but the words wouldn't come.

"His condition is extremely serious. He is presently comatose and on life support. We are still resuscitating him aggressively, and he's already had a couple of emergency surgical procedures here in the ER. He may be on his way to the operating room shortly depending on the results of his CT scans. I need you to be aware that based on what we know so far about his condition, there is a very strong likelihood he may not survive."

As the tears started trickling down Laura's face, Dr. Esteban reached for a box of tissues on a nearby table and set it before her. He sat silently across from her, seemingly unsure of what to do or say next. After a couple of minutes, he cleared his throat.

"You won't be able to see him while we're actively trying to stabilize him—but as soon as there's a chance you can, I'll come back and get you. Is there anything I can do for you right now? Anyone I can call? We'll be happy to assist you in getting in touch with a friend or family member. I could also call in the chaplain, if you'd like."

Laura shook her head, her mind still reeling.

"Alright, Mrs. Young," he said, rising from his seat. "I'll escort you back to the waiting area for now. And I'll come and find you as soon as I have an update on your husband's condition."

"I need a moment," she whispered between sniffles. "I'll find my own way back, thank you." As he departed, she took out her phone and dialed her mother's number.

When Laura finally got a chance to see Will, forty-five minutes later, it was shortly before he was whisked off to surgery. It was as if there had been a savage knife fight in the room, followed by a shoddy, rushed attempt to clean up the aftermath. There were partially open linen bins stuffed with bloody surgical gowns and drapes, as well as trash cans packed with crumpled disposable paper and plastic materials. A few streaks of blood were still visible on the floor where the doctors and nurses had tried their best to clear the mess before exiting the room to make way for the cleaning service.

Will's entire body was swollen, and there was a plastic tube in his mouth that connected him to a ventilator. There were also a number of larger tubes—Laura could see blood oscillating back and forth in them—emerging from both sides of his chest, attached to drainage canisters. She observed his chest rising and falling at regular intervals. There was a big plastic collar around his neck, which he probably would have found to be uncomfortable if he'd been awake. On the screen above his bed was a graphic array of colored lines, each with a distinct recurring pattern that scrolled from left to right. She recognized the cardiac tracing; it seemed to be cycling regularly with a number next to it that ranged between ninety and a hundred, which, along with his breathing, confirmed that he was alive—which wouldn't have been obvious otherwise.

Rina, Will's nurse, was the only one in the room when she was shown in by a nurse's aide. Dr. Esteban must have been too busy to take her, since Laura had passed him on the way. He was sitting at a desk with two other doctors who seemed to be intent on discussing something they were studying on a pair of computer screens.

"They're getting ready to take him to the OR right now," Rina explained hastily to Laura, "after which he'll go to the intensive care unit. Once he leaves here, you can go up to the family waiting area of the Trauma ICU, where they can reach you for updates. Be sure to make your presence known to the nurses in the unit so they know to call you when he arrives from the OR."

When Laura's mother arrived, she waited with her during the long stretch that followed. But about eleven o'clock, Laura urged her to go home for the night, promising to call her if there were any significant developments.

She had curled up and fallen asleep on two armchairs she'd turned around to face each other in the otherwise deserted waiting area, when she heard the ping of an elevator door opening. That was followed by the sound of several voices and the rolling wheels of a gurney. Clambering out of the chairs, she went quickly towards the hallway with her shoes half-on, and caught sight of about six or seven hospital personnel surrounding a gurney they were pushing. Laura watched as they went through the entrance to the ICU and the double doors swung shut behind them. She picked up the telephone receiver hanging on the wall—as she had been instructed to do earlier in the evening—and waited. It rang twice before someone answered.

"Trauma ICU, this is Melanie. How may I help you?" To Laura's ears, the woman's voice was disconcertingly jovial and energetic for two thirty in the morning.

"Er . . . this is Mrs. Young. I was checking to see if my husband is back from the OR. I saw them bring someone in just now, but I didn't know if it was him."

"Hold on one second, Mrs. Young, let me check," Melanie said. A few seconds later she came back on the line. "Give us about ten minutes to get him settled in, then one of us will come out and get you."

When they finally brought her in to see him, he looked about the same as he had before. His whole body looked bloated and he was comatose, with tubes of all shapes and sizes that seemed to emerge from all parts of his body. He was covered in bandages.

One of the doctors came into the room to give her an update, but he used so much medical jargon that she was none the wiser when he was through with his lengthy explanation. While he seemed like a kind and well-meaning person, she felt a lesson in how to communicate in plain English would have been an effort well rewarded. After he left, Laura stood at Will's bedside and touched his hand. It was cold.

"Long night, huh?" said Ellie, his nurse. She was an elderly overweight woman with gray hair and kind eyes.

Laura nodded.

"Do you have any questions for me?" she asked.

"Um . . . so what happens now?"

"For now, we just wait. I don't know if you understood anything of what Dr. Mills said. He's a brilliant doctor and he'll make an excellent surgeon when his time comes, but he's still working on simplifying the complex thought processes in his head so that regular folks can understand him. In a nutshell, your husband's doctors are concerned about whether he sustained any brain damage from the accident, and whether he injured his spinal cord. They'll know more over the next twenty-four to forty-eight hours. Dr. Connelly—the doctor in charge—will give you an update in the morning, after he completes his morning rounds. We'll be getting some follow-up CT scans as well, so he'll be able to brief you on those findings as well."

Laura continued standing by Will's bedside, glancing back and forth from her husband to the monitor above his bed, as Ellie busied herself with drawing blood samples, adjusting intravenous drips and administering a variety of medications.

"If I were you, I'd go ahead and lie down on that recliner next to the bed," Ellie suggested. "There's a couple of blankets there for you, as well as some pillows. Not the coziest of accommodations, but it will do. I'll wake you up if there's any major change. You need all the rest you can get, because there will probably be a lot to do and discuss once daylight comes."

Chapter Eight

LAURA WAS AWAKENED by a soft voice repeating her name several times. She had been dreaming about taking kayak lessons, when she'd suddenly found herself drifting away from the shoreline where her fellow students and instructor were waiting for her. But no matter how hard she tried to get back to them, the current kept pulling her farther out. The instructor was calling her name from the shore, gesturing for her to paddle harder.

"Mrs. Young . . . Mrs. Young . . . Mrs. Young . . ."

She awoke with a start, initially confused about where she was. But once she spotted the hospital bed, she remembered, and was flooded with painful emotions. Ellie was gone, and there was a new nurse in the room—she was the one who'd been calling her name.

"Hello, Mrs. Young, my name is Tricia. I'm going to be your husband's nurse today. I'm sorry to have awakened you, but Dr. Connelly, the attending physician, was hoping to update you on your husband's progress whenever you're ready. There's a sink over there, if you want to splash some cold water on your face, as well as some washcloths, a toothbrush and toothpaste I put there for you."

Dr. Connelly was a tall, gray-haired man with a placid demeanor. He led her into a small conference room at the far end of the ICU, and they sat down at a table already equipped with a box of tissues that made her recall her conversation of the previous evening with Dr. Esteban.

"My name is Peter Connelly," he began, "and I'd like to bring you up to date on your husband's condition."

There was a soft knock on the door. When it opened, Tricia poked her head in. "I'm so sorry to interrupt, Dr. Connelly, but Dr. Young's parents and brother just arrived and they were hoping they could join the meeting."

Dr. Connelly looked at Laura, and she nodded her okay. Inwardly, she cringed.

"Send them in," he rejoined.

Although almost ten years had passed since she'd met them, which was the only interaction they'd ever had, Will's parents hadn't changed much. His father was dressed in immaculately pressed khaki pants and a dark green golf shirt, casual and unassuming, yet leaving no doubts about his station in life. Mrs. Young wore an elegant purple and white print dress with high heels, and the scent from her expensive perfume filled the room the minute she entered. Duncan, Will's brother, came in last, dressed in a tee-shirt, shorts and sandals, a pair of sunglasses perched atop his head.

"We're sorry to barge in," Judge Young said, addressing the doctor, "but we thought it might be easier for you if you could tell us all at once."

"Hello, Laura," said Mrs. Young stiffly, as she and her family seated themselves around the table.

Laura mumbled, "Hi," with marked indifference.

As Dr. Connelly began speaking, he seemed to stare at Judge Young as if he was studying his features. "Hey, aren't you Skippy?" he asked hesitantly.

A huge smile broke out on the judge's face. "I thought your face looked familiar! Peter Wilson Connelly—how have you been all these years?"

"Very well, thank you. Now, isn't that a coincidence! I thought the name William Young had a familiar ring to it when I was reviewing your son's hospital records earlier this morning."

The two men were undergraduates at the same university at the same time, and had played recreational basketball together on a fairly regular basis. Will's father was one of the few black students at the school at that time. But these pleasant moments swapping memories had to be brief, on account of their mutual awareness of the somber business at hand.

"Unfortunately, William is in very serious condition. As you are all aware, he was involved in a motor vehicle accident yesterday, and he sustained multiple life-threatening injuries, including a fractured pelvis, thigh bone and left arm, as well as a lacerated liver, a ruptured spleen and eight broken ribs. So far, we've transfused him with twelve units of blood, in addition to plasma and platelets. He is somewhat stable now—if I dare use that word—relative to his condition when he arrived in the emergency room yesterday. But he has a long way to go, and there are two issues we're especially concerned about at this time.

"One is that he may have sustained significant brain damage because he remains in a deep coma in the absence of any sedatives. The CT scan of his brain didn't show any obvious damage, and we may need to do additional imaging in the coming days if there are no signs of improvement. With each passing day that he doesn't wake up, the likelihood increases that he'll remain in his current state permanently. The second, and equally troubling concern, is that he fractured four vertebrae in his neck, which are the bones that surround and protect the spinal cord. This makes it quite likely that even if he does wake up, he would be quadriplegic, that is, paralyzed from the neck down for the rest of his life."

There was a shocked gasp from Will's mother, while his father remained silent and stoical. Duncan winced. Laura felt tears welling up in her eyes and reached for the box of tissues.

"Isn't there anything you can do to get him better, Dr. Connelly?" Mrs. Young pressed, "and don't worry about the cost! If we have to go to the best hospital in the country for his type of condition, we're ready and willing to do it."

Dr. Connelly shook his head, a look of regret on his face. "I'm afraid there's no hospital anywhere with a cure for a brain injury or a broken neck. Plus, he's too unstable to transfer anywhere at this time. The best we can do at this point is to maintain him on life support and wait to see what develops."

Mrs. Young was beginning to hyperventilate; she was clearly distressed and dissatisfied with his answer. "But doctor, are you even certain about what you're describing?" Her voice had gotten louder, as she became somewhat confrontational.

"Time will tell, Mrs. Young," Dr. Connelly replied calmly. "I'm more certain about the injury to his spine than I am about his brain function, but I sincerely hope for young William's sake that I'm wrong on both counts."

"I hope you're wrong too!" she said in a condescending tone. "Because if the best I can hope for my son is that he'll be a total cripple, then he is as good as dead—and maybe we should spare ourselves the agony and take him off life support now."

Laura felt a flash of anger and defiance course through her body. "Nobody's taking my husband off life support!" she exploded, to the total surprise of everyone in the room, most of all her mother-in-law.

After a brief, stunned silence, Dr. Connelly regained control of the conversation. "No decisions need to be made at this time, although in view of his critical condition, it would be helpful to think about what William himself would have wanted done, given the possibility that he may not get better, and could even get worse. Since he isn't able to speak for himself, his wife should be the one to speak on his behalf. Families don't always agree on what to do in a difficult situation like this one, but I hope—should that time come—all of you will be able to speak in one voice."

After some additional discussion that included Judge Young and Dr. Connelly exchanging contact information, the meeting was concluded. As the doctor rose and left the room, Laura quickly followed, not wanting to be left alone with Will's family.

〜〜〜

Laura was confused about what to do. She didn't like Will's mother, and if there was any silver lining in her reflections, it was the fact she hadn't had to interact with her in the years that had elapsed since their first meeting. Still, she'd brought up a fact Laura herself hadn't considered—what if Will survived, but emerged severely crippled? What would their lives be like then? Up until now, their marriage had been barely functional and not particularly enjoyable, at least not in recent years. That phase of their life was starting to look a lot less complicated than what lay ahead. What if he remained in a deep coma and never woke up? What then?

She was surprised at how much she cared about him now, given how far they'd drifted apart emotionally prior to the accident. At one point, she'd grown weary of being just another planet in the narcissistic universe he'd constructed around him, where he was the glorious sun, around which everything else revolved. He always

80

seemed to consider only what he wanted, often overlooking the possibility that she might have a stake and an opinion different from his. What surprised her was how he always seemed genuinely bewildered when she expressed her disapproval.

Laura stayed in Will's hospital room for a few hours that morning. His family came in about half an hour after the meeting and stood at his bedside, conversing mostly with Tricia, with Judge Young directing a few questions and remarks to Laura, so that the strained nature of their relationship was not immediately evident.

Duncan stood silently in the background. Occasionally his eyes met Laura's, but it was hard to tell what was going through his mind. He seemed dazed. He'd taken an overnight flight from California, which was probably a contributing factor to his state of mind.

"You all are such a nice family!" cooed Tricia to Laura after the three had left.

Laura mustered a wisp of a smile.

Her mother arrived about an hour later and they sat at Will's bedside for about two hours. She didn't say much, but wore a grave expression like someone at a wake. It felt a little strange to Laura when her mother took her hand in hers. She wasn't usually the hand-holding sort, and Laura couldn't recall another time when she and her mother had held hands. Her mother's hand was thin and bony, and her palm was a bit rough and calloused. Still, it felt warm and comforting to Laura.

"Probably best to go home to freshen up and get some rest," she finally whispered to her daughter.

Laura opened her eyes. She'd been dozing.

"This *would* be a good time to go home and get some rest!" chirped Tricia, echoing the suggestion.

Laura was tired anyway and decided to acquiesce. "But if anything—and I mean *anything*—comes up, please give me a call and I'll come right back," she told Tricia emphatically, hoping to make it clear that all calls were to come to her and not to any other member of the "nice family."

Chapter Nine

THE NEXT DAY, Laura was already standing at Will's bedside when his brother arrived. His mother was expected momentarily, while Judge Young had to be in court all day, but planned to visit afterward. Not much had changed in Will's condition.

"How are you holding up, Laura?" Duncan asked, taking his place on the other side of Will's bed, opposite her.

"Hanging on, just barely," she replied with a weak smile.

He bore a faint resemblance to Will and was the same height, but about fifty pounds heavier, and a complexion several tones lighter. Will looked more like his mother while Duncan took after his father. Prior to the previous day's meeting, the last time Laura had seen him in person might have been in school many years ago, although she wasn't sure of it. But she had seen relatively recent pictures of him.

"How's California?" she ventured.

"Same old—a lot more work than play, at least for me."

"It doesn't seem like you come out this way much."

"No, it's a long trip, although if my mother had her way . . . oh, speak of the devil . . ." Duncan said as his mother entered the room.

"Good morning," she said flatly, looking in Laura's direction. "How is Will today?"

"About the same," Laura said, turning to this morning's nurse, Chip, who was tinkering with the forest of IV pumps at the head of the bed.

"Oh, yes, ma'am, everything's pretty much the same as yesterday," Chip concurred in a loud energetic voice. "A few small things here and there, but no big changes."

"Has Dr. Connelly been by?" Mrs. Young asked.

"I haven't spoken to him today," Laura said.

A long, tortured pause followed, where the only sounds in the room were the rhythmic cycling of the ventilator and Chip shuttling back-and-forth from one task to another.

"Laura, could I have a word with you outside?" came the dreaded words from Will's mother, quite unexpectedly.

Laura felt her mouth go dry and her hands began to tremble. As she circled the bed, heading towards the door, her eyes met Duncan's, where she thought she saw a flicker of embarrassment mixed with dismay. She followed the older woman out of the ICU, into the lobby of the waiting area.

"We knew about your marriage within a month of when it happened . . ." her mother-in-law began.

Laura looked startled, but said nothing, knowing more was to come.

"Public records," Mrs. Young continued, smirking in triumph. "Will should be grateful his father is the person he is, because there was a discussion about whether to continue paying his expensive college tuition, or letting him fend for himself, like the independent married man he was pretending to be. My husband is more easily swayed by sympathy than I am, which I find rather ironic, considering he is a judge. Ultimately, he felt we should just play along and not intrude in your affairs, even though it was at a significant financial cost to us." An elderly couple shuffled past them and Mrs. Young paused until they were out of earshot.

"What are you hoping to get out of this situation?" she asked, her voice barely above a whisper, her face contorted with anguish. "Are you prepared to spend the rest of your life taking care of a severely disabled man or a vegetable in a nursing home? You do realize that those are the only two likely outcomes. You could end up being the widow of a living husband, which may be a lot worse than being the widow of a dead one."

Laura's was dumbstruck. Her face flushed with rage as her eyes filled with tears. Without a word, she spun around and started heading back towards the ICU. But as the trickle of tears grew into a torrent, she turned and entered an elevator that happened to open as she was walking past.

"Going down?" inquired the voice of the only other occupant of the conveyance.

She nodded between sniffles without looking up.

〜

In the days that followed the accident, Laura walked around in a daze. She barely ate, and when she did, everything had the same bland, unappealing taste. When she slept, it was a turbulent, restless sleep, her mind picking away mercilessly at the scabs of the recent events and conversations, sometimes in her dreams, but more often during the long stretches in between, when she was struggling to fall asleep. Much of the time she found herself staring blankly into space, her weary mind fettered by apathy and indecision. Even a decision as simple as getting up to make a cup of coffee in the microwave often involved a lot more energy and determination than she could muster.

The days at the hospital seemed to drag on interminably. After an initial surge of hope that seemed misplaced, there was no further news, either good or bad. Will's bandaged body lay unmoving and unresponsive, completely reliant on the ventilator that emitted abstract signals from a monitor that suggested life, with no other evidence thereof. Laura's long hours at his bedside felt no different from waiting with irrational expectancy for a response from a rock, or a tombstone for that matter.

Duncan returned to California after about five days. She had enjoyed their limited contact. After he left, she was seized with the fear that she might have another moment alone with her mother-in-law; but, fortunately, all of Mrs. Young's subsequent visits had been in the company of her husband. The judge spoke little, and his impenetrable visage didn't harbor much warmth or animation except when he was interacting with his old friend Dr. Connelly. Still, when he addressed Laura, he was formal and polite, and she didn't discern any trace of hostility towards her, which was in stark contrast to his wife's harsh and impatient demeanor.

Seeing no improvement in Will's condition, Dr. Connelly had made it clear that he was becoming increasingly pessimistic about his prospects. He tried—privately—to bring up the issue with Laura, sensing that this was a more suitable approach than trying to engage the family as a whole.

"I don't know what to do!" she answered him between uncontrollable sobs. "I've never had to think about anything like this before!"

On the Saturday following the accident, Laura had just managed to fall asleep after tossing and turning, wide-eyed, for most of the night. She finally fell asleep sometime after five fifteen—which was the last time she remembered looking at the clock. The phone woke her at about eight thirty—it was Dr. Connelly.

"He what?" she mumbled, confused.

Dr. Connelly repeated the information.

"I'll be right there!" she said, tumbling out of bed and scrambling to get into the shower.

She got to the hospital about half an hour after the phone call. Tricia, the nurse who'd taken care of Will on the morning after the accident, was on duty.

"Good morning, Mrs. Young," she said enthusiastically. "Your husband finally opened his eyes this morning, and the night nurse got him to follow some commands when Dr. Connelly's team was in earlier. I just came on duty and haven't been that lucky yet."

Bringing her face close to his, Laura gently called his name. "Will! Will! Open your eyes, it's Laura."

His eyelids fluttered open for a few beats, then closed again.

"Dr. Young!" Tricia called out loudly, "open your eyes! It's really important!"

Will opened his eyes again before drifting off once more.

"Don't worry, this happens a lot," Tricia said reassuringly to Laura. "Patients don't always wake up and do what you ask them. Just like if someone woke you up at three in the morning, you might not be very cooperative either."

"Is Dr. Connelly coming back?" Laura asked.

"I'll page him and let him know you're here. I know he wanted to discuss the plan going forward because he's nearly completed his week of service in the ICU, and he wants to tie up the loose ends before handing Will over to his partner."

Dr. Connelly arrived about thirty minutes later in the company of one of his residents. He was courteous, but got right down to business. "William made a little progress today," he began. "It's not much and I don't know if there's more to come, but I wanted to review the next steps in his care because I'll be going out of town early tomorrow morning and don't want to leave things hanging." He paused thoughtfully, before he went on.

"When I rounded earlier with the team, he opened his eyes and we were able to get him to blink twice and lift his head slightly off the pillow on command. So that definitely tells us that he's in there. We couldn't get him to squeeze fingers or wiggle toes, reinforcing my prior suspicion that he did sustain irreversible damage to his spinal cord and may not be able to move his body from the neck down."

The delivery of what was supposed to have been exciting news, strapped down to the leaden anchor of reality regarding the spinal condition was confusing, even anticlimactic. Laura wondered briefly why Dr. Connelly had called her so early in the morning. He seemed to have read her mind.

"I wanted to get a hold of you before the events of the day start pulling us in different directions, so we can decide on the next step in his care. Typically, at this point, if we're going to continue providing this level of support, we'll need to make a hole in the front of his neck, called a tracheostomy, so we can take the tube out of his mouth and connect him to the ventilator through the hole."

Laura recalled that earlier in the week one of the nurses had mentioned this possibility to her in passing; she'd meant to read up on the subject but never got around to it. She trusted Dr. Connelly. He'd been very candid with her throughout, and he seemed to be a genuinely caring person. Initially, she'd been concerned that he might sideline her in favor of Will's parents; but he managed to seamlessly navigate his roles as old friend on the one hand and professional caregiver on the other. She gave her consent to the procedure, which would be scheduled for the following week. After she made the decision about the tracheostomy, she felt as if a load had been lifted, since the pressure to "do something" that had been stifling her increasingly went away.

"Dr. Connelly?" she called out hesitantly after him, as he and his resident were leaving.

"Yes?" he turned around, with a mildly surprised look on his face.

"Do you think my husband will ever walk again?"

His face fell, and he shook his head. "I doubt that very much," he said softly.

≋

About a week or so after the accident, Will's parents stopped coming in daily and began to visit every three or four days, usually after Laura had left, which she didn't mind. Although they'd exchanged phone numbers early in the hospitalization, there was no need to communicate any information other than the routine updates the attending nurse passed on to them in person.

Besides her mother and Will's family, the only other visitors who'd come to see him were a few of his colleagues from work. Tina was a kind, thoughtful and extremely practical person who, within the first few minutes of their conversation, had pulled Laura aside and in a soft but urgent voice, asked her whether Will had an insurance policy for long-term disability benefits, and whether she'd given thought to what she would do to adjust to the potential loss of her household's primary income earner. She seemed genuinely concerned and wasn't at all intrusive with her questions, and Laura felt comfortable talking to her—especially since she hadn't given even a passing thought to any such considerations.

Along with Tina, there were two younger women—Aisha and Audrey. They both looked stunned and horrified when they saw Will lying comatose, attached to a ventilator. Audrey was accompanied by her boyfriend, Matt, and she sought solace from the distressing sight by pressing against his side, while he draped his muscular tattooed arm reassuringly around her shoulder.

Tina came back for a second visit a few days later. She was alone this time. Once again, after inquiring into the details of Will's condition and prognosis, she launched into another discussion advising Laura on next steps. She also brought news from their human resources department regarding Will's salary and benefits. It was decided that he would receive his pay through the end of the month, after which the company would make short-term disability payments for a period of three months—part of their standard benefits package—in addition to covering his medical expenses. After that, he would cease to be an employee of Iatros. Tina delivered this final piece of news with a grave expression, as if it was tantamount to death.

Meanwhile, Laura was feeling relieved to hear about the three-month buffer period, which she hadn't counted on. Still, heavy storm clouds were building on her financial horizon. She discovered that Will wasn't entitled to long-term disability benefits. With only her income, she wouldn't be able to afford the house, so she'd already decided she'd have to sell it. Tina had given her the names of a couple of realtors she knew personally who she thought would be able to help. As Laura struggled to sort through the gobbledygook of crucial information, a random thought came to her mind unbidden that this whole mess would have been a lot easier to manage if Will had died. She shuddered at the thought, and quickly chastised herself, but not before wondering if this was the same calculation that her mother-in-law had made on the day of their first briefing with Dr. Connelly.

Chapter Ten

"I HOPE THAT'S the last ride for ol' Ms. Tomkins," declared Spencer as he let out a deep sigh of exasperation. "That lady's been trying to get out of this purgatory for a mighty long time!"

"Mmm . . . mmm . . . mmm," echoed Lucretia, nodding emphatically, "now, that be the truth! She be tryin' to die for a good long while!"

The short-lived clamor that had accompanied the arrival of the ambulance team at the skilled nursing facility died down, and most of the staff who'd come out into the hallway to take a peek returned to their tasks. The two orderlies, Spencer and Lucretia, returned to the main nurses' station and sat down, although it was clear that neither of them was ready to resume what they'd been doing before the emergency call was initiated.

The two were an odd pair—a frequent fixture at the nurses' station—engaged in constant conversation whenever there was a relative lull in their activities. Spencer was a middle-aged white man with a scraggly beard and tobacco-stained teeth; he had a booming voice and a distinct southern drawl, which was most notable when he pronounced words like "time" and "try"—which sounded like *tahm* and *trah*. When he was in a good mood, numerous eruptions of his harsh, explosive laugh could be heard, even in instances where the humorous element was difficult to discern. Today, he was not laughing. Lucretia was a petite woman—barely five-feet tall and almost seventy years old. Despite her age, she worked with relentless energy. Her ebony skin was remarkably devoid of wrinkles. She had an unshakeable equanimity—never appearing overly excited, even when there was good reason to be, which was quite the opposite of Spencer.

"That's the fifth time we've sent that poor soul back to the hospital in the past two years! When is it gonna be time to say enough is enough and let her go? Eighty-eight years old, just lying there, not doing much of anything, except getting bedsores . . . and that son of hers that keeps threatening the doctors at the hospital and telling them to do everything to keep her alive . . . he never comes here to see her . . . I mean . . . when was the last time you saw him coming to visit her?"

"It wa' last Thanksgiving," Lucretia replied without hesitation, "I know 'cause I be keeping count. Almost ten months now. And from what I hear, whenever she go to the hospital, he show up immediately and raise hell, telling everybody what to do and pretending that he care about her. I don't know why he do it. Maybe it 'cause he collecting her social security . . . you never know with some o' these people."

Spencer gritted his teeth and his eyes flashed angrily. "I already told my wife and kids. If I ever had a big stroke like Ms. Tomkins, they need to leave me the hell alone and let me go in peace. I don't wanna end up in no place like this, being fed through a plastic tube, collecting sores on my butt . . . that ain't living!"

A middle-aged woman entered through the sliding doors and greeted them warmly before proceeding down the hallway to room number ten. They both smiled at her and acknowledged her greeting, waiting until she was out of earshot before resuming their conversation.

"She special, that one," Lucretia opined.

"Mm . . . hmm, she's in a league of her own. Must be the hardest thing to have to come in every single day and see your son like that and know that he will never get better."

"I don't know how she manage."

The woman in question had a twenty-five-year-old son who'd been involved in an accident about four years earlier. He'd gone swimming in a creek with a few friends in his college class, having been a third-year student at one of the local universities at the time. Somehow, amidst the fun and excitement, he'd drifted a short distance away from his friends to where the water suddenly became much deeper. Initially, when his friends saw his hands waving above the surface of the water, they thought he was goofing around. They weren't aware of the sudden drop that made the water so much deeper there and the current significantly stronger.

When his hands disappeared beneath the water, they became concerned and scrambled in his direction. It took them about ten minutes to retrieve him. By that time, he was about twenty yards downstream from them—having been dragged away by the current—and had it not been for two of his companions who were very strong swimmers, he would have been lost. A less skilled swimmer than they were would have been swept along with him. Another friend, who'd been watching the rescue effort from the riverbank, called an ambulance that arrived quickly. The paramedics came on the scene to find his friends trying to resuscitate him, apparently to no avail.

Despite aggressive treatment at the hospital, the victim was left with severe and permanent brain damage, only able to open his eyes, grind his teeth, and moan and groan intermittently. Before the accident, he'd been among the top students in his class, and was planning to go to medical school after completing his undergraduate education.

The victim's mother was in her mid-fifties, but the incident had clearly taken a toll on her. Her hair was almost all gray, and worry lines had taken up permanent residence on her face. She had a quiet, resolute demeanor, and visited her son every day. She spent anywhere from two to six hours at his bedside, speaking to him softly and holding his hand. All the nurses liked her since despite the tragic circumstances of her life, she was invariably kind to them and knew most of them by name. She never raised her voice, even when she was unhappy about something the staff should or shouldn't have done.

"I don't know what would happen to that young man if she were not here," Spencer said to Lucretia, his voice cracking unexpectedly with emotion. "That's just too difficult to think about."

A somber pause followed, with both of them returning half-heartedly to the tasks they'd been attending to before the distress call came from Ms. Tomkins' nurse. Sometimes it was easier to get through the workday without asking the obvious hard questions that were on everyone's mind.

Patrice, the nurse in charge, stopped by their station a short while later.

"We're getting a new arrival this afternoon," she announced quickly, trying to head off a revival of Spencer's rambling tirade about Ms. Tomkins, which she knew was coming, since most of the staff had heard a version of it more than once in the course of the preceding two years.

"Oh," exclaimed Spencer, "that was fast! Are they going to take ol' Ms. Tomkins' room?"

"No, this one's going to the vent unit. It's a young man—a doctor actually—who was involved in a car accident about three weeks ago and is paralyzed from the neck down. They're hoping that eventually he'll be weaned off the vent, although it's a fifty-fifty chance . . . there's no harm in hoping, you know."

Spencer half-swore, catching himself before the entire

unseemly word had escaped his lips. His face and neck flushed scarlet. "Oh, man! There's no shortage of depressing news in this place, is there?" he muttered.

"Somebody's got to take care of these folks, Spencer," she replied with a smile. "It gets to me sometimes too, but it's not the patient's fault for needing to be here."

"I disagree, Patrice," he growled testily. "I think in Ms. Tomkins' case, it is entirely her son's fault for not letting her die. We've watched her body rotting away slowly, piece by piece."

Patrice did not reply. She glanced knowingly at Lucretia. It was best not to engage Spencer head on when he was having one of his ill-humored moments.

"So, who gonna take care of the new patient when he come in this afternoon?" asked Lucretia.

"Keturah."

"Oh, good for him. She the best! What time's he coming?"

"About three."

"Keturah is awesome!" remarked Spencer unexpectedly, the frown on his face melting away.

"Mm . . . hmm, she never get mad."

"Actually, Lucretia, that's not completely true. There's a day she heard me referring to this place as a junkyard. Oh man! She was not happy, and she let me have it. She said to me in that deep island accent of hers: 'Spencer, this is not a junkyard, and these people are not junk.' I can't say it the way she said it, but man . . . I felt really stupid after she chewed me out."

"I think she's from Africa, not the islands," corrected Patrice.

"Well, whatever . . . all I know is that day I saw a side of Keturah that I had never seen, and never want to see again."

"Remember the old demented guy who used to be in room fourteen?" Patrice continued. "You know, the one who kept swinging at the nurses and getting up at night trying to get out of this place. Remember him?"

"Oh, yeah—old man Dudley, I remember him! He was a nice guy when he wasn't acting crazy, which was pretty much only when he fell asleep from being worn out from all the energy spent being a pain in everyone's behind."

"He was very different when Keturah was taking care of him," Patrice observed. "He'd be sitting nice and proper and answering 'Yes, ma'am' and 'No, ma'am' to her. I remember walking past the room once and thinking I was in the wrong hallway—the one where the other guy, Mr. Peters, is. You know how they kind of look alike and their rooms are the second room on the right. I had to walk back and check the room number to make sure I was in the right place."

"I think he had a crush on her," chuckled Spencer, "that's the only way I can explain it, 'cause he was messed up and then some. She probably figured out that if letting a crazy old man have his crush was what it took to keep him calm and polite when she was around, then that was probably worth it—as long as he didn't try to grab her or anything."

Patrice glanced at her watch. "I need to head over to the other side to see how they're doing. You guys try to stay out of trouble and give me a holler if you need me," she said.

"Alright, but if there's a vote to be had, I'd say we give out ol' Tommie's room and not hold it for twenty-four hours like we did the last time. Maybe if there's no room for her here, then her soul is gonna have to find a new resting place, if you catch my drift."

Patrice rolled her eyes. "I'll see you all later," she called over her shoulder as she started to walk away.

〰

Laura arrived at St. Matthew's, the skilled nursing facility, about an hour after the ambulance took Will there. The facility was housed in an older building situated in the midst of a lush landscape of carefully tended trees, shrubs and flowers. The floor plan was in the shape of an upside-down "T," so that on entering the main lobby one could head left, right or straight ahead—or take the elevator and do likewise on the upper floor. After the sunny exterior, everything seemed dark inside to Laura; but in a few short moments, her eyes adjusted to the indoor lighting. When she came to the reception desk, she asked for directions to Will's room. She was told to go down the right-hand hallway, all the way to the end, where she would find his room—C20.

Once she got there, a nurse opened the door to leave and stopped abruptly in the doorway when she saw Laura. She was short, about five foot two inches, half a head shorter than Laura, with a stout physical frame. Her jet-black irises matched her skin tone, making the white part of her eyes stand out even more, especially in the somewhat dimly lit hallway. Her face wore a serene expression that seemed at odds with the circumstances. On her right nostril was the lustrous gold orb of a nasal piercing. When she smiled, which she did the minute her eyes fell on Laura, her immaculate white teeth came into view, so that if the room were dark enough, only her eyes and teeth might be visible.

"Oh, hello," she said warmly, "were you about to go in here?" Her voice was high pitched, and marked by a buoyant confidence.

Laura nodded.

"Would you mind telling me who you are and your relation to the person in there?" She said this in a pleasant tone of voice, and almost teasingly; but from the way she stood blocking the doorway, Laura knew that her answer to the question would determine whether she would gain entry or not.

"I'm Laura Young, and I believe the person in there is my husband Will, who was brought in here a short while ago."

"Alright . . . I was just making sure you're in the right place, that's all. My name is Keturah, and I'm your husband's nurse. I was on my way to the nurses' station, but I'll be back shortly."

Laura thanked her and stepped into the room, which was a lot larger than it had seemed when she'd been around to tour the facility before deciding which one to choose. It had big windows and a brighter aspect than the hallway and lobby areas. When she looked through one of the windows, she was treated to an expansive view of the well-kept flower gardens and shrubbery.

Will was lying in his bed with his eyes closed, the only sound in the room being the quiet ebb and flow of air to and from the ventilator. After that first day when he'd reportedly opened his eyes and seemed to interact with Dr. Connelly's team, his progress had been spotty. He seemed to have fallen back into a deep slumber, seldom interacting with his environment. The neurology team had been called in to assess him; and after running numerous tests they came back with nothing, advising that the best thing to do at this point was to wait and see. Occasionally there was a report from the night nurse that he had opened his eyes, but he never did more than that; and the reports always seemed to come from a junior nurse with the event happening in the wee hours of the morning, making it difficult to surmount the ever-rising wall of skepticism in the minds of those who spent long days, Laura included, watching eagerly for a sign that things would get better.

When Keturah returned, she and Laura chatted amicably as

she shuttled back and forth in the room from one task to the next. She had an easygoing personality and a good sense of humor, and Laura quickly became comfortable around her. As she spoke, Laura found herself enchanted by her mellifluous accent, which was about as unusual as her name. She scrutinized her name tag surreptitiously at one point during their conversation, and was embarrassed to find Keturah's gaze fixed on her when she looked up, even though she hadn't skipped a beat as she'd been talking.

"Whoops! You caught me. I don't mean to be a nosey parker, but I'll die of curiosity if I don't ask you what country you're from—I was trying to figure it out from your name," Laura explained awkwardly.

"My first name or my last name?" Keturah asked matter-of-factly.

Laura just blushed. She didn't know what to say.

Keturah grinned. "Nobody ever knows what to say when I ask them that. My last name, Omondi, is from Kenya. Everyone assumes Keturah is a Kenyan name, but it's not—it's from the Bible."

"Really?" Laura exclaimed in disbelief. "But I've never once heard that name mentioned."

"Well," Keturah said triumphantly, "one day, when you have some time, look up the story of a man called Abraham. After his wife

Sarah died, he married a woman named Keturah who had six sons with him."

"Wow!" said Laura. "I'm just so surprised I've never heard that name before. I know the Bible is full of weird names . . . oh, I'm sorry, I didn't mean to imply that your name was weird or anything . . ."

"That's okay, every name is weird to someone else living in a different place, time or culture. There's nothing wrong with that."

Laura, an intense, puzzled look on her face, was still fumbling through this odd discovery. "So . . . I'm sorry to keep asking you personal questions, but what's the meaning . . . I mean, do you know the meaning of your name?"

"It means incense, or fragrance."

"I like that!"

"What does Laura mean?" Keturah shot back.

Laura was momentarily speechless, then laughed sheepishly. "Now that you mention it, I've just realized I don't know what my name means. That seems absurd considering I'm asking you about yours."

"Actually, it's not that unusual. I think the more common your name is, the less likely you are to ever ask yourself, or have someone ask you, what that name means. If you doubt me, I suggest you find twenty people named John and ask them what their name means, then come back and tell me if I'm mistaken."

"Hmm . . . I never thought of it that way!"

"And while we're on the topic of names and their meanings, may I ask you another question?"

"Sure . . ." Laura replied somewhat hesitantly.

"I noticed that the first letters of your husband's name, William Henry Young, spell the word 'WHY.' Is that just a coincidence or is there a story behind it?"

Laura grinned, the solitary dimple on her left cheek coming into prominence. "Apart from me, you're the only other person I've met who's made that observation unprompted. When Will and I met in middle school—long before I ever knew or suspected I'd be his wife—that was one of the things about him I noticed immediately. When I asked him about it, he gave me this blank look and said he wasn't aware of it, and that no one in his family had ever mentioned it either. There was no intended meaning, as far as I know, although I can't tell you how many times I've found myself asking the question 'why' in the last few weeks . . ." Her voice trailed off as her eyes became moist.

Keturah said no more. Giving Laura a gentle sideways hug, she returned to Will's bedside and resumed her duties.

Chapter Eleven

LAURA FOUND SELLING the house something of an adventure. The first realtor Tina had recommended was someone named Mr. Lucas. He'd seemed like a nice enough individual when she met him at his office to discuss some preliminary details. But when he came over to view the property, she started having second thoughts. He was a thin, balding middle-aged man with the urgent, boisterous manner of an over-caffeinated squirrel, his eyes darting to and fro as he made pronouncements regarding the sale with an air of absolute certainty.

"Oh, this house is way too big! Way too big, I say!" he announced to her the minute she opened the door to let him in. When he stepped inside, he started mumbling to himself as he looked around. "Big houses are a nightmare to sell nowadays. Nobody wants these anymore. And they're even harder to put on the rental market!"

Laura said nothing, but her heart sank.

"Show me around," he said in a commanding tone, humming tunelessly to himself as he started walking towards the kitchen ahead of her.

She followed him silently, scrambling within to regain her composure.

"Where's the water?" he demanded.

"The what?" she asked, puzzled.

"The ocean," he said impatiently.

"Oh, the beach is just beyond those dogwood trees over there," Laura said, pointing in their direction.

He let out a deep sigh. "That's going to be a problem too. You see, ten or twenty years ago everyone wanted a house by the water. But with the way the oceans have been rising, nobody wants to get too close. This will definitely impact our ability to sell competitively."

Laura's heart sank further, but again she said nothing.

Mr. Lucas proceeded to open one door after another, peeking into rooms, peering out through windows, muttering abstractedly to himself as if he was making mental calculations. When he'd completed his tour, he sat across the dining table from her, and gave her his verdict.

"Your house is going to be a tough sell, especially because it's already October, and there's a number of strikes against your property—but we'll see how it goes. Our best bet would be to go in with a selling price that's about five to ten thousand dollars lower than similar properties in the area to make up for the negatives. The last thing you want is to put it on the market and have it stay there for a long time, because, as the saying goes, the longer it stays, the longer it stays!" He said the last part with a dry, mirthless chuckle, although it appeared he might have been expecting her to find it amusing.

She stared blankly at him. "I'm going to have to think about this. I'll get back to you after I've weighed my options."

"Very well, but don't wait too long. It's only going to get more difficult as you go into November and December!" he called over his shoulder as he went down the front porch steps to his car.

After he left, Laura let out a dejected groan and debated for a while about calling the other realtor whose number she'd been given. Finally, she went ahead and made the call, setting up an appointment for the following week.

Lisa Cummings had a distinctly calm demeanor, and didn't smile or say much. Her gaze was unyielding when confronted by another's, and the serious expression never left her eyes. She seemed like someone who might make a great ally without necessarily being a friend. After a routine walk-through of the house, she asked just a few direct questions before she was ready to discuss her plan for the sale.

"This is a good size house in a great neighborhood close to the ocean. October is probably not the best time to sell, but people buy houses when they need them, and everyone's needs and time frames are different," she observed.

"Do you have any other concerns besides the time of year?"

Laura probed.

"Not really," she replied, shaking her head slightly.

Lisa put the house on the market the following week, and Laura began looking for a house in Magnolia Circle. She'd grown up in that part of town and spent most of her weekends at her mother's house now, so it was a natural choice. The houses there tended to be much smaller and older than where she currently lived, and some were located on sites that were run-down and unsafe. But there were also some nicer areas where the residents had lived for decades, where everyone knew everyone else and looked out for each other. Even if Will was never able to work again, she could afford to make payments on a house in that neighborhood. Deep down, she felt like this was where she always belonged.

With the housing problem solved, Laura felt she was finally making some significant progress with her life since Will's accident—until another bombshell dropped. It was when the first monthly invoice for the car payment arrived and she learned what type of car Will had bought. Her eyes almost popped out of their sockets when she saw the amount of money that was due. "Two thousand dollars!" she shrieked in disbelief. "What on earth were you thinking, Will? How am I ever going to pay this?"

The car had been completely totaled, and the insurance people were still in the process of determining how much money they would pay out. There was no telling how long it would take them to complete their assessment, and the car payment was due in a week. Without thinking about what she would say, Laura picked up the phone and dialed the number on the invoice. When she heard a voice on the other end, she stammered out, "Er . . . hello, I just got a bill for a car payment and I wanted to see . . . uh . . . if there was . . . like . . . see, my husband got into an accident with that car the same day he bought it. He was very seriously injured and we're not even sure he's going to survive. So right now, I'm trying to figure out . . ."

"Ma'am?" the woman interrupted.

"Er . . . yes."

"I'm sorry to hear about your husband, but the loan still has to be repaid. If you don't mind holding, I'll put you through to Mr. Wilkins, who deals with situations that involve extenuating circumstances. Let's see if there's anything we can do to help you. Please hold while I put your call through."

Laura inhaled nervously as she waited for Mr. Wilkins to come on the line. After a minute or so, she heard a voice almost feminine in pitch. She went on to explain the reason for her call.

"I'm very sorry to hear what happened to your husband, Mrs. Young. Now here's what I'm going to ask you to do. Please put down everything that happened in writing and drop it off at our office. I'll also need a letter from your husband's doctor confirming your account of the events that transpired and his current condition. Given the limited amount of time between now and when the payment is due, dropping off the documents in person would be the surest way to get things moving. We may be able to extend the due date for the first payment for up to thirty days, but I do need you to realize that the loan will still have to be repaid in full. I don't know where the insurance people are with their inspection, and how much money you'll receive from them, but regardless of that, the amount borrowed will have to be paid in full." There was a brief pause before Wilkins added, "Is there anything else I can do for you?"

Laura, still dazed from the shock of discovering how much money Will had borrowed for the car, replied in the negative and thanked him for his time. Even though he'd gone off without her to buy a new car, it had never crossed her mind that he would be so foolish as to buy one that cost a hundred and twenty thousand dollars—especially without first discussing the matter with her. And ironically, the car cost about the same as a house in Magnolia Circle.

♒

Samir was originally from Jordan, and when he spoke, he did so in slow deliberate phrases infused with a heavy Arabic accent as well as a lisp, which may have accounted for his aversion to the use of spoken English. It would have been easy for someone who didn't know him to perceive him as rude. The permanent sagging at both corners of his mouth was often mistaken for a scowl, and didn't make for a favorable first impression. All the hair on his head was white, and his tanned face was crisscrossed with wrinkles. Still, it was difficult to guess his age beyond estimating he was somewhere between sixty and eighty years old. He'd worked at St. Matthew's for almost twenty years, and was one of only three remaining employees who'd been present from the day the facility first opened its doors.

"Hey, Samir! I haven't seen you in a long time," Keturah called out with a big smile as he came into Room C20.

He nodded calmly in acknowledgment, and a rare twinkle came into his brown eyes. He stood quietly by the ventilator and dialed in some adjustments to the settings.

"Do you think he'll be able come off the ventilator?" Keturah asked.

"Only God know," Samir said as he shrugged, before muttering his favorite expression, "I'm just therapist."

Keturah smiled to herself as she logged into the bedside computer and started typing in her assessment. She glanced surreptitiously at the ventilator screen as Samir monitored Will's respiration. "He breathed on his own for about eight hours yesterday," she remarked to Samir. "That's pretty good."

Samir nodded, after which a comfortable silence ensued, as they both focused on their work.

"Why he not wake up?" Samir suddenly asked her.

Keturah was startled at first by the unexpected sound of his voice, and didn't answer him immediately. Instead, she became thoughtful. "You know, besides taking account of the damage from the accident, I don't think they ever found a good answer for that. I heard that he woke up initially but not since, and the MRI didn't show extensive brain damage."

Samir scrutinized Will's face, glanced at the ventilator screen, and then turned and left the room without another word.

After he left, Keturah pondered his question since it had occurred to her too. Will had been at St. Matthew's for about two weeks, so she'd expected that by now he would be showing more signs of recovery. Sometimes, when she was close to him, she noticed his eyelids fluttering, almost as if he was trying to open them. But when she said his name and tried to get his attention, he didn't seem responsive.

His wife came in every day for a few hours, and Keturah enjoyed their conversations. She knew her well enough by now to sense that Laura was silently beginning to despair about her husband's apparent lack of progress. She used to ask her every day whether there'd been any improvement, but recently she'd stopped asking. If the subject of his condition happened to come up in the course of a conversation, Laura's voice would begin to quiver and she'd immediately talk about something else.

Will's parents had visited a few times while Keturah had been on duty. His father seemed resolute and unemotional. She found him polite to a fault, but noticed he had difficulty with small talk, like when he ventured questions about herself and her job. Will's mother didn't say much, and it was clear that it bothered her immensely to see her son comatose and hooked up to a ventilator.

The day wore on somewhat unremarkably, with Keturah moving back and forth between her two patients' rooms. The patient in C19 was an eighty-year-old man with dementia and swallowing problems who was receiving nutrition through a feeding tube implanted in his stomach. Most of what he said was completely unintelligible; but unlike many in his situation, he was completely calm and never tried to take a swing at the nurses or climb out of his bed without assistance.

She'd just finished getting Will cleaned up with the assistance of one of the nurse's aides and was washing her hands at a sink facing away from the bed, when she began to have a strange feeling, as if she was being watched. She felt the hairs on the back of her neck stand up and her whole body was tingling. Still lathering her hands with soap as she stared down into the sink, she stepped casually to the right and positioned herself at an angle to the mirror, then suddenly looked straight up. Their eyes met in the mirror, as she felt a frisson of fear and excitement run through her. Keturah turned around.

"Well, it's about time you woke up, isn't it?" she said, trying to sound calm. Her mouth was dry and her heart was pounding in her chest.

Will's eyes were cold, brooding and distant. He kept his gaze on her as she walked towards him, then closed his eyes again.

"William! William! Please open your eyes again!" she urged. "It's really important for your assessment."

The eyelids fluttered a little but didn't open.

Keturah was puzzled. Had he been awake all this time? The look in his eyes was not the usual vacant look of someone tumbling in and out of consciousness—there was someone in there! As hard as she tried to get Will to respond to her again, she couldn't bring him back to the state he'd been in a short while earlier.

Laura arrived at about four o'clock. Initially, Keturah planned to tell her about the new turn of events, but then changed her mind. She watched Will's face carefully as Laura sat by his bedside, holding his limp hand and speaking to him intermittently. His eyelids were still.

By the time Laura left, Keturah was confused and frustrated by the situation. She had about an hour to go on her shift. There was still daylight coming in through the windows, so she turned off the overhead lights to give her eyes a rest. Sitting down next to Will's bed, still warm from Laura's body, she let out a heavy sigh. "It's been a long day, William. I've been on my feet continuously for the past nine hours, so it's a relief to be able to finally sit down." As she spoke, she studied his face, and saw his features fixed in inanimate repose, like a death mask. Besides the rhythmic rise and fall of his chest in sync with the ventilator, there was no other sign he was alive or conscious. "I wonder what you're thinking, if you're in there," she mused aloud. "You probably have a lot of questions about what happened and how you ended up here."

The tranquil glow of the setting sun colored the boxwood shrub outside the window orange, while rays of light spilled into the room, which was starting to darken. A couple of birds were hopping about playfully on the bush, casting long shadows on the floor. For Keturah, the combined effect was peaceful, and she smiled to herself and began to hum. She had an unusually beautiful voice that could start from a deep, mournful place, and climb effortlessly up the musical scale to high-pitched crystalline notes—and just as easily move down again. As she hummed, her mind flitted aimlessly from one random thought to another, until there was a knock at the door.

"Come in!" Keturah replied, as she got up from her seat and turned on the light. It was Trevor, coming on for the night shift.

"Oh, hey, Keturah! I heard singing, so I figured you must be in here, although I had second thoughts about that when I noticed the lights were off."

"Well, I turned them off initially to enjoy the calming sunset; then as it got darker, I didn't want to get up and turn them on while I was serenading my good friend, Dr. Young, here. It's all part of a nurse's job description, you know."

Trevor looked over at the recumbent figure. "How did he do

today? Any change yet?" he whispered to her anxiously, looking rather concerned.

She shrugged and shook her head.

"That stinks!" he exclaimed, still keeping his voice down. "I hope this isn't what the rest of his life is going to be like. I feel sad for his wife." As he watched Keturah getting ready to leave, his eyes brightened suddenly. "You know, you should consider a career in music. I think I've told you that before. Not that you're a bad nurse or anything, but you have a really good singing voice."

Keturah grinned awkwardly. "Oh, I don't know," she replied with a shrug. "I'm happy where I am. Besides, there's probably not that many good songs left to sing."

Chapter Twelve

SAMIR THOUGHT IT odd the next day when Keturah asked him for a Passy Muir valve for the patient in C20. This was a small plastic device that, when placed at the opening of a tracheostomy tube, transformed unintelligible whispers into audible words, sometimes to the surprise of the speaker who might have gone several weeks without hearing their own voice.

"How he talk if he not wake up?" Samir asked, looking perplexed.

Keturah bowed her head and didn't answer.

He watched her briefly, waiting for her to speak or look up at him. As he did, a familiar mixture of pain and tenderness overwhelmed him, and his eyes misted over with tears. Keturah reminded him of Safiya, his daughter, who'd been gone almost ten years. Not a night went by when he didn't think about her. He remembered the first time he met Keturah—five years before when she'd first arrived at St. Matthew's—he felt inexplicably drawn to her. It was only after their third or fourth interaction that he finally realized why: it was when he inadvertently called her by his late daughter's name. Keturah smiled, but didn't correct him.

Safiya had been slender, about a head taller than Keturah, with beautiful brown eyes and the most perfect set of small white teeth. She was the most cherished treasure of her father's heart, reminding him of her mother, Hanan, who'd died during childbirth. From the time she was a little girl, it was as if she knew her presence was a precious balm on her father's soul, and the two were inseparable. For Samir, her death had been more difficult to deal with than Hanan's, probably because he'd always cleaved to her for consolation after his wife's death, and never expected he'd have to bury her too.

"I just try to understand so I can help you," he pressed on awkwardly.

Finally, Keturah looked up and smiled at him. "I want him to be able to speak from the minute he opens his eyes, Samir. He's making so much progress with his breathing." Will had been off the ventilator for a little over two days, although he still remained largely unresponsive to the world around him.

Samir came back into Room C20 about twenty minutes later carrying a small boxed package. "Must always deflate trach balloon when putting it on valve," he said firmly. "Call me when ready and I put it in, okay?"

"Yes, Samir," she nodded. About ten minutes after he left, Keturah picked up the package and inspected it, then broke the cellophane wrapping around the box and opened it. She looked down at Will's face. "Hey, buddy, open your eyes. It's time you and I had a conversation."

His eyelids fluttered slightly, but didn't open.

She popped open the container with the valve and inspected it, then glanced at the illustrated instructions that came with it. Without hesitating, she positioned the valve over the opening of the tracheostomy tube.

"Okay, William, it's time to wake up and talk," she coaxed him.

Suddenly, Will grimaced and his eyes opened, but he looked like he was choking, while beads of sweat broke out on his forehead. Keturah panicked and looked around frantically, wondering what was wrong.

It was then that Samir appeared at the door, as if he'd been summoned telepathically. He strode quickly to Will's bedside and yanked the valve off his tracheostomy tube. Will's head fell back onto the pillow, the grimace vanished as his facial features softened, and his eyes closed again. But his breathing was still rapid and labored.

"He choke!" Samir said sharply. "Why you not deflate balloon?"

Keturah buried her face in her hands as her eyes began to well up with tears. "I'm so sorry, Samir! I completely forgot about the balloon."

"Why you not call me to put for you?" he said, his voice straining with irritation.

"I'm sorry," Keturah murmured.

Samir shook his head in dismay as he was leaving, but turned around when he got to the door. "You make him better. He nearly wake up from choking," he quipped with a wry smile, "better than not wake up at all."

〰

Laura's life had become a frenzied blur, as she untangled one knotty problem after another in the new reality that she was living since Will's accident. She'd made the monthly mortgage payment on the house from their savings, but that would soon run out if she continued spending at the same rate. The house was on the market and had been shown a couple of times without clinching a sale, but it was too early in the process to start actively despairing. Having the house ready at short notice for potential buyers meant she had to confine herself to the bedroom and the kitchen when she was home. So, most days, she left early in the morning and didn't return until late at night. Sometimes she chose to spend the night at her mother's, preferring the cramped overly intimate quarters to the large empty house, where her anxious thoughts were amplified and echoed like ghostly whispers, especially when the lights went out and a gloomy silence overtook the reassuring background noise of daily activity.

Mr. Wilkins, the financing liaison for the car dealership had, as promised, managed to delay the first payment on the car; but the thirty-day grace period was coming to an end. The insurance people were still hiding behind a screen of opaque jargon with regard to recovering the cost of the car, saying they would let her know when the process had been completed. Her workdays at the school seemed to have become more hectic as well, probably because she had less time in the evenings to keep up with her lesson plans as a result of everything else she had to deal with. The principal had suggested she take a leave of absence, but she declined, preferring not to free up large amounts of time for gratuitous, unrewarding nail-biting.

After she resumed work, she visited Will in the evenings, between six and eight o'clock. With time, the monotony of sitting next to his inanimate body—separated from death only by the mindless ebb and flow of air from the ventilator and the cryptic repetitive scribblings of his internal organs on the monitor—had started to wear on her. She began to feel she was there only out of a sense of duty, which engendered feelings of guilt and shame. After the almost impudent certitude with which she had defied her mother-in-law's suggestion at that first meeting with Dr. Connelly, ever-widening fissures of doubt had appeared.

Laura had seen Will's family a few times since he'd been moved to St. Matthew's. His father was predictably impassive, to the point where it had become a reassuring quality. But it was disturbing to take note of how rapidly he seemed to have aged in the past two months since the accident, even developing a slight stoop in his posture. His eyes wore a lost, dazed expression, as if he'd finally come across a case where his power as a judge—to make a decision one way or the other—was useless to him. All he could do was wait helplessly for an outcome beyond his control, which was probably the same place many of his defendants inhabited as they awaited their sentence or the outcome of their appeal. There were new streaks of gray in Mrs. Young's impeccably coiffed jet-black hair, and she seemed to have run out of the energy to engage in the overbearing hostility that had characterized her earlier interactions with Laura.

On this particular evening, it was about six thirty when Laura arrived at St. Matthew's. There was a noticeable chill in the air, with the sun setting earlier as autumn set in. As she approached the main entrance of the building, she saw two familiar figures heading into the parking lot.

"Mr. and Mrs. Young!" she called out hesitantly, overcoming an impulse to continue past them as if she hadn't seen them.

They looked in her direction as she approached. "Oh, hello, Laura. How are you today?" Mrs. Young said in a crisp, formal tone.

They stumbled through a rudimentary conversation, with Laura's mind at every turn racing to figure out what to say next to avoid any painfully awkward pauses. This challenging task had become somewhat easier with practice. She learned that Duncan would be visiting again soon, and had asked them to pass along his regards when they saw her. After he returned to California, they'd not heard from him much, although one day Laura had been awakened at three in the morning by a surprise text message from him. It simply said, "Hey Sis, thinking of you. Be well."

She'd read it several times, her mind focused on the one word "Sis." It stirred up feelings of affection mixed with a degree of discomfort, since she wondered if she understood it the way he'd intended. Was it a casual term he used routinely in informal exchanges with women he knew; or had he meant it in the way she hoped, as a term of endearment for the wife of his only brother? After much thought, she simply texted back, "Thanks so much!"— waiting to send it about nine am California time so as not to wake him up.

"By the way, has the car insurance issue been sorted out?" Judge Young asked, before they parted ways.

Laura was surprised at the question since she didn't recall ever discussing the matter with her in-laws. Also, these were the only words he uttered during the entire encounter, otherwise listening silently and nodding as she and Will's mother conversed.

"I'm still waiting for them to get back to me," she said with a sigh. "The process seems to be dragging on and on."

As Laura hurried into the foyer of the building, she was thinking about what her mother-in-law had just told her, that Will had reportedly opened his eyes earlier in the day. They hadn't observed it themselves during their visit, but the daytime nurse, Rodney, assured them he'd witnessed it, and said Will had remained that way for a number of hours. Despite what seemed to Laura like great news, her in-laws exhibited no signs whatever of encouragement or excitement, as if they didn't want to cash in their nearly depleted emotional reserves on fanciful speculation.

Rodney was in his mid-twenties and muscular, with elaborate tattoos of Chinese calligraphic characters on both arms. While his head was clean-shaven, he sported a thick well-trimmed beard and mustache, as if the hair on his head had whimsically decided one day to migrate to the lower half.

"You just missed his parents," Rodney said as Laura walked into the room. "They left about ten minutes ago."

"I ran into them outside in the parking lot, and we talked for a little while," Laura said. "How's my husband doing today?"

"Well, he opened his eyes for me earlier in the day—for a couple of hours. I haven't taken care of him for a week or so, so that's a new experience for me."

"Did he seem like he knew where he was?" Laura said anxiously.

"It's hard to say, especially because he's a quadriplegic. You can't ask him to squeeze your fingers or wiggle his toes, you know what I mean? He seemed to be looking at me, since I could see his eyes following me as I crossed the room. But what that means in terms of his overall prognosis is a question only his doctor can answer. Let me see if I can get him to do it again."

Rodney went and stood close to Will's bed and bellowed in his ear, tapping him repeatedly on his shoulder. "Hey, buddy, could you open your eyes? I have a visitor for you."

There was a hint of a grimace on Will's face, then his eyelids fluttered open.

"There you go!" declared Rodney triumphantly. "Look, Will, your lovely wife is here to see you."

"Hey, Will," Laura said excitedly, leaning over the railing of the bed. "It's me, Laura. I'm so happy to see you waking up!"

His expressionless eyes turned towards her, but there was no sign of recognition.

"Will! It's me, Laura!"

His gaze drifted from her to Rodney, then up to the ceiling before turning back towards her again.

"Will, do you know where you are?" asked Rodney.

Will's lips started to move, but no sound came out. Laura got closer to him and with desperate concentration tried to make out what he was saying. He seemed to be saying the same thing over and over. She looked up quizzically at Rodney.

"Don't look at me," said Rodney. "I'm awful at lipreading!"

As she struggled to read his lips, Will seemed to become

angry as his efforts became more emphatic and yet were frustrated.

"Will," Laura said gently, "please repeat it slowly and I'll try to follow along. Say the first word again . . ."

He repeated the first word.

"I . . ." she echoed.

He nodded.

"Okay, I got the first word. Go ahead and say the next word slowly."

He whispered the next word rather forcefully, causing a rush of air through the opening of his tracheostomy.

"You . . . ate? Are you trying to say ate?"

Will rolled his eyes and shook his head.

"No, not ate, but something close. Let me see . . . hate, maybe?"

He nodded, and as he did, the color started to drain from her face. His eyes were cold and spiteful, and suddenly she knew what he'd been trying to say. As if to make certain she'd understood him correctly, he slowly and deliberately mouthed the three words again: "I hate you."

Laura felt her body go numb, and instinctively she took a step back from the bed. Fortunately for her, she was spared the embarrassment of Rodney's witnessing this interaction. He was mentally preparing for his evening handover, so luckily his mind was elsewhere.

"Are you leaving already?" he asked in surprise as he saw her moving towards the door.

"Yeah, I need to get going, I have a long day tomorrow," she mumbled dejectedly, still reeling from what had just happened.

"Well, it looks like he's made quite a bit of progress today," Rodney rejoined. "They might even be able to put a speaking valve on his trach tomorrow so he can communicate more clearly. Wouldn't that be great! Have a good night, then."

"You too," she replied as she exited the room.

Chapter Thirteen

THE HOUSE SOLD in mid-November, and she wearily moved their belongings into a rental house located about a quarter of a mile away from her mother's. She reckoned she would live there for a while to allow time for the dizzying chaos to subside. She'd found her mother not altogether enthusiastic about the idea of her moving to Magnolia Circle; and once she got into the habit of stopping by her house every two to three days, she began to understand why.

One afternoon, after ringing the doorbell twice to no avail, Laura decided to go around to the back in case her mother was outside gardening. As she opened the side gate and walked past the trash cans, she noticed a cardboard box containing about six or seven large gin bottles—all of them empty. Familiar feelings of anger and helplessness suddenly surfaced, and once again she was an angry, frustrated teenager locked up in her room, tears flowing freely after another emotionally draining verbal showdown with her sullen, red-eyed inebriated mother. Most people became jovial when they got drunk—but not her mother. She would sit wordlessly at the kitchen table, a resolute scowl on her face as she lifted the glass to her lips, taking one sip after another, pausing occasionally to refill it when it was empty.

"Mom, you don't even look happy! What's the point if you're not even having a good time?" Laura had blurted out once with the smug all-knowing self-confidence of a sixteen-year-old.

The verbal cudgeling that followed ensured that would be the last time Laura overtly critiqued her mother's drinking. Instead, she tried to introduce the subject in more subtle ways only when her mother was sober and in an apparently good mood. But more often than not, it put an end to any pleasant conversation that had preceded it. Since she'd moved back to Virginia Beach, Laura had gotten the distinct impression that her mother had cut back on her drinking, but now—after seeing the numerous empty bottles—she thought it might have been only wishful thinking.

Not finding her mother in the garden, Laura knocked on the back door. Initially there was no response, but after a second knock and a pause—just as she was preparing to walk away—a silhouette appeared in the living room and shuffled towards the door. It was her mother, still in her night clothes, her face clenched into a tight frown from the bright sunlight.

"Hi Mom. I'm sorry, I didn't realize you were sleeping. It's two thirty in the afternoon," said Laura, trying not to sound reproachful.

Her mother shrugged and mumbled, before retreating back into the kitchen as Laura followed her inside.

"Coffee?" she offered, as she placed two mugs on the countertop and then tossed a used filter laden with wet coffee grounds into the trash can.

"Thanks." Laura didn't really feel like drinking coffee, but now she felt obliged to after having intruded on her mother's day.

After setting up the coffee to brew, Ms. Sullivan went into the living room and opened up the curtains wide, before coming back to sit in one of the rickety chairs at the small dining table. "So, how is he doing?" she asked her daughter.

Laura wondered why she never seemed comfortable referring to him by his name. "He's about the same," she said with a sigh. "He seemed to be waking up at least a little bit when I saw him a couple of days ago, although I'm not sure if that means anything. I didn't get to see him yesterday since I've had so much going on with the move. But I'll probably pay him a visit tonight."

It had actually been more than a couple of days since Laura had visited Will, after her upsetting encounter with him the last time. Every evening since then, she'd managed to come up with a sound excuse, which was easy to do in the midst of moving.

"Mmm . . . that's odd," Ms. Sullivan murmured to herself as she placed a mug of steaming coffee in front of her daughter. She sat down across from her and took a sip from her own.

"What's odd?"

"You've been going to see him every day for the past couple of months, and then when he finally begins to wake up, you don't have enough time to see him?"

Laura blushed, and her lips quivered nervously. "Well, he's

not really awake, in that sense of the word," she countered hastily. "Besides, I'll see him today, so what's the big deal?"

A long silence ensued, in which Laura squirmed uncomfortably. Her mother had an uncanny ability to read between the lines and pick up on what was not being said. Unlike someone more sensitive who, when discerning an inconsistency, would let it go unnoticed to spare the other person the embarrassment of a cross-examination, Ms. Sullivan came right out with her uncensored observations.

"Are you going grocery shopping today?" Laura pivoted. "I'm going to need to pick up a few things, so we can go together if you like."

"Sure, why not? I just need about twenty minutes to get washed up, then we can go. I could even come with you later to the nursing facility—it's been a few weeks since I saw him."

"No, that's fine. I wasn't planning on a long visit today, so there's no need to drag you across town. We could probably go together next week instead," Laura added quickly.

≈

Will had been much easier to deal with when he was comatose, Laura thought ruefully. Prior to the accident, he had been thoughtless and insensitive towards her; now he was downright cruel. As much as she wanted to believe it, she knew what he'd said to her last time hadn't been a mistake. As she reluctantly pushed open the door to Will's room, she could hear Keturah chatting with him at the top of her high-pitched voice.

"Oh, hello Laura!" she called out excitedly, pronouncing her name in a way only she did, so it sounded something like Low-rah. Her brilliant smile and effervescent manner stood in stark contrast to the rock-hard malevolent countenance of the other occupant of the room; and from the look on Keturah's face when she looked back in his direction, the change had just occurred.

"Where have you been?" Will said in a low snarl.

Laura's whole body went numb and her face turned ashen. She stood motionless in the doorway, unsure of what to do or say.

"William!" Keturah admonished. "That's not the way to talk to your wife, is it?"

He turned and glared at her, then flopped his head back on the pillow and stared at the ceiling, a sullen expression on his face. For what seemed like a very long time, no one spoke, until Keturah broke the silence.

"William, what's wrong? We were having such a good time."

He glanced briefly at Laura as if in response to the question.

By this time, Laura's body was shaking uncontrollably as a rising sense of indignation boiled up inside her. Seeing no other recourse, she was preparing to back out of the room, when she heard Will's voice.

"You should have let me die!"

"William, stop . . ." Keturah protested.

"No, you stop and listen to me!" he countered. "Why did she let them keep me alive? Look at me now—crippled and laid up in a hospital bed. Is this what you were hoping for, Laura? Huh? Is this what you wanted all along?"

"William, please! How was she to know . . .?" Again, Keturah tried to intervene on Laura's behalf, but to no avail.

"Oh, like she didn't know that my spine had been injured? Didn't you tell me a few days ago that my spine was injured during the accident?"

"But William, how was she to know what you wanted? She made the best decision she could with the information she had at the time. Did you ever tell her before the accident that you would never want to be kept alive if you had a spinal injury?"

Keturah's irrepressible generosity of spirit, almost child-like in its ability to identify silver linings, had finally come up against an impenetrable, insurmountable barrier of negativity. She seemed to be struggling to regain her footing, and the more impassioned she became in her efforts, the more bilious and accusatory Will became in his condemnation of Laura, until she'd had enough. She stepped backwards and gently pulled the door shut, escaping the notice of both Will and Keturah who were completely absorbed in their argument. As she headed down the dimly lit hallway towards the exit, Laura was surprised at how she'd managed—to all outward appearances—to maintain a sense of calm throughout the entire episode.

Chapter Fourteen

YEARS OF BEING abused and repeatedly let down by the callous, self-seeking adults in his world had left festering emotional sores on Elias Mundy's soul, squeezing out all vestiges of the carefree childhood that his classmates still enjoyed. For a nine-year-old, Elias was remarkably cynical and cruel. To alleviate his own inner torment, he constantly sought to inflict pain on his fellow classmates. He did it with feral efficiency, sensing weakness that wasn't apparent to others, and never missing an opportunity to pounce, subdue and humiliate. From a stealthy shove aimed at an unsuspecting classmate, to a shocking outburst of anger and obscenity, one way or another, he kept everyone around him on edge. The only time the other children felt at ease was when he skipped school, which was not an infrequent occurrence.

Laura strove to keep him contained by trying to ignore his bad behavior and eagerly bestowing effusive compliments when he somehow got things right. For the most part this had worked, though the fact that she expended about half her energy on any given day trying to restrain him, meant that the other twenty-eight students had to be content to share whatever was left over. They seemed to intuit that it was in their best interest if he behaved himself, since when he was out of control, nothing much got done.

As one of the newer teachers at the school, it was no surprise to Laura that he'd ended up in her classroom. The other teachers had managed to carefully steer him away from theirs since they were already aware of his tendency to foment mayhem. He came to the school the previous year when he'd transferred there from North Carolina, midway through first grade. He'd already been suspended twice for yelling and throwing objects at the teacher, a pattern of behavior that matched one of the reasons he'd left his former school. His mother had been summoned on a few occasions to speak with the principal, and from the reports of those who'd met her, she was every bit as ill-humored and unpleasant as her son.

Laura had so far been able to tolerate Elias, while comfortably suppressing any latent frustration or animus by reminding herself constantly that she had to do that to maintain his trust, if she wanted to rescue the wretched boy from his self-destructive folly. But on that particular day, he had sensed a chink in her emotional armor and had readied himself to pounce. Maybe it was the way she fumbled abstractedly through the lesson plan, or the way she snapped unexpectedly at the soft-spoken and perpetually diligent Sarah Johnson, the perennial teacher's pet. Whatever it was, Elias saw something that signified an opportunity to inflict pain, and he moved in for the kill.

Laura ignored his repetitive yawning and bored expression as the class read through a storybook. When he threw a paper airplane across the room, she pretended not to have seen it even though it landed a couple of feet from her desk. And when the diminutive

Roger Philips, who sat in front of Elias, squealed suddenly and turned red, but refused to say why, she just went along. The more Laura ignored him, the bolder and more determined Elias became, until, as the class quietly listened to Morgan Smithson dutifully stumbling through a passage she'd been asked to read, a deafening thud rent the air. Loud gasps of consternation ensued, as everyone in the room turned in the direction of the sound. Elias' desk was toppled over and books were strewn on the floor. He was sitting in his chair, half-smiling and half feigning surprise, making it clear to Laura that this wasn't an accident. She snapped.

"Elias Mundy, put that desk back right now and come with me! We're going to the principal's office!" Laura was yelling at the top of her voice, and her face was infused with a crimson hue. The other students were wide-eyed with a mixture of fear and fascination since they'd never heard her raise her voice before. Elias, on the other hand, sat smugly in his chair, not making any effort to rise, as if challenging her to deliver the "or else" that was implicit in her commands.

It was difficult to tell how much time actually elapsed during the standoff. To Laura, it seemed like an eternity. She was feverishly taking stock of her limited options, and was beginning to realize there wasn't much she could do to save face if he refused to move, since physically trying to remove him would open up a Pandora's box of unintended consequences. But she was so enraged that she started rushing over to him, a murderous expression on her face.

Suddenly the door swung open and the principal, Dr. Sinclair, appeared. She was a tall, lean bespectacled woman in her late fifties with a graying pixie haircut and an incurable fetish for order and discipline. She happened to be passing by when she overheard Laura uncharacteristically raise her voice.

"You!" the principal said in a fierce, but hushed voice, pointing a long bony finger at Elias, "Get to my office right now! And pick up that desk like she told you to!"

Elias seemed jolted out of his irreverent stupor and hastily scrambled out of his seat, proceeding to do as he was told. Laura escorted him out of the classroom as he followed in the direction of Dr. Sinclair's receding figure. Then she managed to find a teaching assistant to mind her class, as she too went to the principal's office to sort out the incident.

Elias' mother was irritated when she received the phone call requesting her immediate presence at the school. Like the previous times this had happened, she had a hard time understanding what all the fuss was about, insisting that her son was being picked on. She strode into Dr. Sinclair's office with a combative attitude in her stance, pushing open the door without knocking first. Laura was startled, but Dr. Sinclair seemed unfazed, as if she'd been expecting it.

Dorothea Mundy was a petite woman, but she had wild, threatening eyes, and she flailed her heavily tattooed arms around as she spoke, which made her seem larger and more menacing than she was already. "What's going on with my son?" she asked angrily.

Dr. Sinclair calmly explained what had happened. As she spoke, Ms. Mundy sighed, couldn't seem to stand still, and occasionally rolled her eyes until she finally couldn't contain herself any longer.

"Is that all you called me here for, or is there something else? So my son's desk toppled over—accidents happen. I don't understand why y'all are making such a big deal out of it. Just like I said the last time, I think you're picking on my son and looking for ways to get him in trouble."

"Nobody's picking on your son, Ms. Mundy, but we cannot allow him to continue being disruptive to the other students."

The repeated rolling of her eyes indicated an unbridgeable gulf in perception. Dr. Sinclair, usually unflappable, was starting to get a tad agitated. There ensued an unproductive exchange of accusations until the principal held up her palms and shook her head slightly with an air of finality.

"Listen Ms. Mundy, this discussion is going nowhere. As of now, Elias is officially suspended from school for the next two days. In other words, he shouldn't show up here either tomorrow or the day after."

A scornful expression formed on Ms. Mundy's face. "So, no

school for the next two days? Is that all? Is that why you called me away from my job? Couldn't you have just given him a note for me at the end of the day, saying he was suspended? I shouldn't have to leave my workplace just so you can tell me he shouldn't come to school for the next two days. I've been trying really hard to keep my job, and y'all should be able to deal with stuff like this without forcing me to take time off work."

"Ms. Mundy," Dr. Sinclair replied, the pitch of her voice rising slightly, "your son has been suspended for serious behavioral infractions, and if this pattern continues, he could end up being expelled from this school."

"Whoa, stop right there, lady! Did you just threaten me?" Ms. Mundy countered angrily. "Listen here, and listen good—don't you *ever* threaten me! You don't know me! I will make your life miserable! If you continue harassing my son, I'll find myself a lawyer and sue you. And I'll report you to the school board and make sure you lose your job—you and this dumb redhead wannabe teacher of yours!"

As Dr. Sinclair rose to her feet in indignation, Ms. Mundy stormed out of the office, determined to have the last word, grabbing her son who'd been waiting outside and undoubtedly overheard the entire exchange.

Laura remained standing in the corner of the principal's office, speechless and bewildered.

"Hopefully that'll give you an idea of where the young lad is coming from," Dr. Sinclair remarked in a half-whisper, as she picked up a folder and prepared to leave her office, indicating to Laura the meeting was over. "And it might amaze you to learn that this confrontation was probably the least explosive of the three I've had with her!"

〰

Laura hesitated when she saw an incoming call from the same unfamiliar number that she'd ignored twice the previous day. The caller hadn't left a message, leading her to conclude that it was probably a telemarketing call. Why she changed her mind and answered this time was a complete mystery to her.

"Laura . . . hello . . . this is Keturah," said a familiar voice on the other end of the line.

She frowned in surprise at first, then artfully managed a smile as she tried to infuse some enthusiasm in her tone, while her mind raced anxiously wondering why Keturah was calling.

"I hadn't seen you in two weeks, so I was just calling to see how you're doing."

"I'm doing great, Keturah—how about you?"

"Oh, you know, everything's fine."

Laura was tempted to ask her how Will was doing, if only to move the conversation along, but she really wasn't interested in talking about him. As a matter of fact, with each passing day since her last visit to St. Matthew's, she'd managed to push him further and further away into the periphery of her daily thoughts, which seemed to be working out pretty well so far for her peace of mind.

"So, are you going to be visiting us anytime soon?" Keturah asked innocently.

All things considered, it was an odd question. But knowing Keturah as she did, Laura understood it the way it was intended. Keturah would always refer to Laura's visits to the nursing facility as "coming to visit us," as if the staff and patients at St. Matthew's were family members whom guests came to visit. Laura guessed that this notion derived from Keturah's cultural background.

"Oh, I don't know, Keturah. I have a lot going on, and the last time I was there, things didn't go so well."

"Yes, I remember it well. William can be difficult sometimes."

"Well, Keturah, thank you for checking up on me. That's very kind of you," Laura said graciously, having concluded at this point that it was time to end the call since there wasn't much of a basis for fruitful discourse.

After a long pause, Keturah said bluntly, "Laura, I'm leaving—that's actually why I called. Tomorrow is my last day."

"That's certainly sudden. I didn't know you were planning to leave. Are you taking another job in the area?"

"No, I'm moving to Oklahoma. I have a friend there who's recently divorced, and she has a fifteen-year-old special-needs son. She's having a difficult time putting in the hours at work and taking care of him at the same time. She needs her job to pay her bills. And her son hasn't been doing so well since her husband abandoned them."

"That's very generous of you, Keturah. She's very fortunate to have you for a friend. Is she a nurse too?"

"No, but she often has to work nights for her job, so it will help her to have someone to watch her son when she does."

"Well, I hope all goes very well with your move, and with your new life. I appreciate all the excellent care you gave Will. You're a special kind of person, Keturah. Thanks for calling to say good-bye." As Laura hung up the phone, she reached for a tissue from her handbag and began to dab at the stealthy drops of moisture that had formed unexpectedly and were starting to trickle down her face.

Chapter Fifteen

THE DAY AFTER Keturah left, Will had become an intolerably irritable and obnoxious patient. In addition, he demanded a new nurse—dismissing the allegedly incompetent Elisa, a soft-spoken new hire with pretty brown eyes and a heart of gold. In fact, after tending to Will and bearing the brunt of his dark mood, she'd needed an hour of intense emotional rehab administered by two of the older nurses, as the fragile edifice of her self-worth came crashing down under the weight of his patently unjustified hostility.

Leah, the nursing supervisor, may have been smiling deviously on the inside when she assigned Joe B to take over Will's care, but if she was, it would have been impossible to tell from her even-keeled, no-nonsense demeanor. Joe B was about six foot five and weighed about three hundred and fifty pounds. He was reputed to have been a fearsome defensive tackle in his college football days, although no visible vestiges of his athletic past remained. Years of alcohol consumption and an unfettered lust for carbohydrates padded away the hard edges and muscular contours, so he now resembled a larger-than-life teddy bear.

Joe B spoke little and tended to mind his own business, his massive frame being a sufficiently persuasive argument against those who considered getting in his way. Occasionally—and often unpredictably—he would erupt into a short-lived paroxysm of fury, sending all those around him scattering towards the exits. Then, like a mid-summer coastal thunderstorm, the terrifying clamor of passion and vexation would vanish as suddenly as it had come, and it was safe to be around him again.

Joe B was slow and deliberate in his tasks, and somewhat absent-minded at times—not exactly a stellar worker but one who reliably showed up every day. Nobody knew where the name Joe B had come from, although it seemed like a reasonable assumption that at some point in the past there may have been a Joe A, because neither his last or middle name began with the letter "B."

Will knew that Leah had dropped the joker on him the minute Joe B entered his room. After politely acknowledging his arrival, he let out a deep sigh and then settled in for a long, quiet afternoon. He was starting to drift off to sleep when there was a soft knock on the door before his parents appeared. Joe B excused himself and went to check on his other patient.

Will's parents hadn't visited him in about three weeks. The last time they stopped in was when he woke up from his coma—the day he told Laura he hated her. While they had seen him awake and somewhat interactive the previous time, he was now completely lucid and able to converse using the Passy Muir valve. As he watched them approaching his bed, he pondered the situation briefly, and decided to proceed with the plan he'd been churning over in his mind. "I need a lawyer," he said without preamble.

Judge Young just went on with what he was doing as if he hadn't heard his son, pulling up chairs so he and his wife could sit closer to the bed. Will knew his father well enough to recognize in the slow, methodical arranging of the chairs that he was analyzing what had been said and formulating a careful response. Mrs. Young sat closer to Will's head, while the judge, ever the gentleman, waited until after his wife was seated before sitting down himself.

"How have you been?" This from his father.

Will nodded and said he was okay.

"When are they planning on taking out that thing?" his father asked, pointing at the tracheostomy.

"Hopefully soon. The respiratory therapist has been pretty happy with my progress, and plans on discussing it with the doctor when he comes around next."

"Why do you need a lawyer?" his father finally asked.

Will felt a twinge of embarrassment. The brief detour had dissipated his initial sense of urgency. Still, he managed to blurt out, "I want a divorce."

His mother gasped in surprise, then quickly fixed her gaze on the floor. The judge squinted at his son as if to make sure the person he was talking to was who he thought he was.

"A divorce? This seems like an odd time to be thinking of a

divorce," his father said, sounding perplexed.

"I've been thinking about it for a while, and I see no reason to put it off any longer."

"And, er . . . Laura, what does she think of this idea?"

"She hasn't been here in over two weeks. I told her not to come anymore." Well, not in so many words, he thought.

An uneasy silence ensued, during which Judge Young stared resolutely at the blank wall on the opposite side of the room, while his mind spun with discordant thoughts. Mrs. Young sat stiffly with a frown on her face, tightly focused on suppressing the one or two unkind thoughts about her son and his intentions, that had just popped into her mind. Glancing sideways, she caught her husband's eye, and a slight nod exchanged between them signaled an agreement to abbreviate their visit.

"So, if you got a divorce," asked the judge, "where would you go when the time came for you to leave this facility?"

Will was silent. It wasn't clear whether he'd gotten this far with his plan.

"Before I forget, Duncan says to say hello," added his father, deftly changing the subject.

"Is he coming soon?"

"He said he might in his last call, but he hasn't decided on a specific date yet."

An uncomfortable pause ensued.

"Well, we need to get going now," Judge Young said, as he and his wife got up to leave. "I'll ask Timothy Lacroix, one of my trusted lawyer friends, to come see you, and you can tell him what's on your mind."

〜

Timothy Lacroix was balding and lanky, a soft-spoken individual with intense gray eyes, who'd been a protégé of Judge Young in the early years of his career. He was now one of the senior partners of Felton, Sykes, Ellis and Lacroix LLP, the premiere law firm in the Tidewater area, with imposing offices in Norfolk and Virginia Beach. When his mentor called him with his somewhat unusual request, he promised to get right on it, and said he considered it a privilege to be able to help.

Tim was an unassuming individual who was on a first-name basis with all the lower-level staff members in his office building— from the parking attendants to the night janitor, people who were often overlooked as mere props in the backdrop of daily life. It was not unusual to catch him commiserating with one of them about an ailing parent or a headstrong teenager hell-bent on self-destruction. They resisted calling him Tim—although he specifically requested it—feeling it to be too presumptuous. Instead, they settled on calling him Mr. Tim, which seemed to resolve the tension between familiarity and respect.

Despite his easygoing and affable nature in these sorts of interactions, Tim had a relentless energy in the way he went about his work, spending long hours poring obsessively over documents and precedents, as if to quell a constant, nagging concern that he might miss something of significance. It was this quality that stood out to Judge Young—still an attorney at the time—when he'd first joined his team fresh out of law school. At the time, many in the practice believed that the new lawyer's ambitions would be seriously stymied by his diffident, unimpressive manner; but the judge had seen something special in him that no one else seemed to have noticed.

Yet despite his initial confidence in him, Judge Young had experienced some second thoughts during his first few months, so that even he found himself awestruck when the young attorney began racking up decisive, seemingly impossible victories against more seasoned litigators. His hesitant, unfocused manner apparently disarmed his opponents, who mistook it for incompetence. Humility was another one of his virtues, since Tim never let his victories go to his head; from winning he derived merely a sense of relief and a sense of vindication—affirming the fact that he'd adequately prepared his case.

Tim showed up at St. Matthew's two days after Will's parents had visited, at about six in the evening. He was walking down the hallway counting down the doors, when he encountered Joe B who was exiting Will's room.

"Um . . . hello sir, I'm looking for Will Young. I believe this might be his room."

"And you are?"

"My name is Timothy Lacroix. I'm a friend of Will's father. We haven't met, but he's expecting me."

Joe B eyed him suspiciously, then motioned for him to wait, as he turned around and went inside the room.

"Hey, there's a white dude in a suit outside, says you might be expecting him," he muttered.

Will nodded.

Joe B went back outside and said to Tim, "You can go in." Then he continued down the hallway in the direction of the break room.

As he entered, he said, "Hello, Will. My name is Tim Lacroix, and I'm a friend of your father's. He speaks very highly of you." As he approached the bed, he remembered not to stretch out his hand in greeting. Pulling up a chair, he sat close to Will—where his mother usually sat—so they were at eye level with each other. "How's everything going?"

"So-so," Will said softly.

"Your father mentioned you might be in need of my services. What's on your mind?"

Will perked up as he began to describe his situation, while Tim listened patiently, without interrupting.

After Will went silent, he said, "Alright, let me see if I understand this. So, it's not anything your wife has done or not done for you following the accident, but rather the general state of things even before it happened?"

"Pretty much," Will affirmed.

"Have you discussed your feelings with her, currently or previously?"

"No, not really."

"Okay." Tim decided that given the unusual and apparently one-sided nature of Will's request, an assessment by a neurologist and probably even a psychiatrist might be necessary, to make sure Will hadn't sustained any residual brain damage as a result of the accident.

"I'll need your permission to obtain your medical records from the hospital, just so I can get an idea of the extent of your injuries."

"Not a problem."

"Has the doctor said anything about your long-term prognosis? Like, for example, is there an expectation you will leave this place at some point, or that you will regain any strength in your arms or legs?"

Will looked thoughtful before responding. "I haven't heard anything from the doctor that comes around, but he's not a specialist, so I don't know how much he'd be able to tell us."

"Okay, but that's information we will need. In fact, we'll probably need to have a more current assessment by a specialist who does evaluations of spinal cord injury patients—I forget what they're called . . ."

"A physiatrist?" Will suggested.

"Yes, that's right. I often get that term mixed up with 'psychiatrist'—not that I think they're the same!" Tim added hastily.

"Well, the words do share a lot of the same letters," Will observed wryly.

Will seemed able to converse so normally that Tim, who'd been studying him closely, was baffled. Something didn't add up. So he decided to be a little more direct. "Listen, Will, obviously it's your right to do what you want, but I'm concerned about the timing. This seems to be a rather odd time to want to call it quits on your marriage. I mean, you have a lot going on already, and divorce proceedings can be very nasty and uncomfortable. I just worry that the timing may not be optimal, given everything else you're dealing with now."

A dark expression drifted briefly over Will's face, then vanished. He was silent for a few minutes more until he said, "I need help with something else too."

"What's that?"

"I'd like to sue the jackass that T-boned me and put me in this situation!"

"Alright, I can certainly look into that as well."

"How long will it take?"

"How long will what take?"

"Getting all that done."

Tim shrugged. "It's too early to tell. Let me look into both these matters and then get back to you. I'll also need to consult some of my colleagues who have more experience than I do in these areas. I'll let you know what I find."

As the attorney rose to leave, Will looked at him like he wanted to say something, but was hesitating.

"Oh, don't worry, Will, there's no charge to you," Tim said, reading his mind. "Your father and I go back a long way. I consider it an honor to be working with you."

〜

Tim mulled over the situation for a few days, but he was having trouble making headway. Part of the problem was he didn't have enough information about the basis for Will's divorce; and he didn't want to set the wheels irreversibly in motion based on a seemingly illogical request from someone who may have sustained just enough brain damage to affect his judgment, while apparently functioning normally from a cognitive perspective. From what Judge Young had told him, Laura was a devoted wife who'd done everything that had been expected of her, so a divorce request seemed a rather odd way of saying "Thank you." Meanwhile, the process of obtaining access to the medical records would buy him a little time to come up with a coherent strategy.

He heard his cell phone buzz inside his pocket, and when he looked at the screen, he saw it was Rupal, returning his call from the previous day.

"Hello there, Rupal—you're one very difficult person to get a hold of!" Tim said jovially.

"Not really, Tim. I'm just difficult to get a hold of if you're in a hurry. I like to slow things down to my pace, and my voicemail is my strongest ally towards that end. We're not that young anymore, you know."

"It's strange to hear that coming from someone who's probably completed their fiftieth marathon since the last time we spoke."

"Fifty-fourth actually, but who's counting."

"Oh well, there you go. I need your thoughts on a situation

I'm trying to sort through."

"Sure, go ahead."

"This involves someone who's a client but not really a client . . ."

"Uh oh, that's never a good beginning, Tim. You should always keep your friends and clients in separate boxes."

"Well, this one's a little complicated and unavoidable for the most part."

Tim explained the situation to his colleague. She was an attorney too, living in Phoenix, Arizona, and a few years his senior career-wise. They'd worked together about twenty years before, when she lived in Norfolk, and she was the one who'd introduced him to Annie, his wife.

After he'd completed his explanation, Rupal let out a sigh. "It sounds like your client-buddy needs to have his head examined. Why would he choose this time to divorce his wife? Even if they had marital issues before the accident, it would not be in his best interests to bring that stuff up now. Not unless she's a wealthy dame. And who's he planning on living with when he's released from the rehab center?"

"I don't think he has a clue, at least he didn't seem to when I talked to him."

"Maybe the accident damaged that part of the brain that makes people think logically? What's that part called? The frontal lobe . . . or whatever it is, I'm not sure—you definitely should have him checked out. Or maybe there's a woman involved, who knows? I would imagine, though, if that were the case, she would have appeared by now, at least in the hospital or at the rehab. Wow, sounds like there's some weird stuff going on in Hampton Roads! Must be the humidity—I could never get used to it."

Tim smiled and let out a soft chuckle. "Maybe so, Rupal, maybe so."

"So, remind me again, Tim, who's this guy to you? I mean, you're in corporate and real estate law. What are you doing getting mixed up in a divorce case? Has business slowed down?"

"No, this one's for a friend. I don't know if you remember a guy by the name of Bill Young. He used to be an attorney back in the day, then he became a judge—although you might have left by the time that happened."

"Of course, I remember Chill Bill, as Sofia used to call him, the guy with the temperament of a block of ice. I remember him—he never got excited about anything, although I remember hearing about that one time when he lost it and yelled at a court clerk. I happened to be in the building at the time, which is why I knew about it. But everything blew over so quickly that the people who witnessed it, including Mrs. Milne, the clerk in question, started to wonder whether they had imagined it. Brilliant guy, I liked him a lot! Oh dear, is that his son?"

"Yup."

"Oh, no, that's terrible. How's he coping?"

"He's probably struggling, but it's hard to know what's going on inside him. He doesn't let on much."

"And how's Mrs. Young? She was one of the prettiest people I've ever laid eyes on! Hair, makeup—everything was just perfect. I remember inviting them to our wedding and hoping that Amit wouldn't look at her and notice how plain his bride was in comparison. Of course, in hindsight that sounds rather foolish, but at the time it seemed like a real thing to worry about. What a classy chick!"

"She's definitely got style," Tim agreed. "I haven't seen her recently, but I would assume she's still doing okay."

"Well, I'm sorry I can't offer you any more insights into this challenging situation, but you're a smart guy—I'm sure you'll figure it out. Maybe the best thing to do is go after the guy who caused the accident and drag your feet a little with the divorce case."

"You know what, Rupal, that's exactly the direction I was leaning towards. Let me go after the low-hanging fruit while I'm trying to figure out what's behind the divorce."

Tim thanked Rupal, hung up the phone and looked up at his wall clock. It was already five forty-five. As he got up to leave, he suddenly remembered Phil Curtis. Phil would have access to Will's accident report, which would be a reasonable place to start digging.

Chapter Sixteen

TIM FOUND OUT what he needed pretty quickly from Phil Curtis. He learned that the accident occurred around eleven fifteen in the morning. Will's car had been hit by a 1980 Ford Ranger truck that had come barreling down a feeder road at fifty mph and blown past the stop sign. It rammed into Will's car on the driver's side, and it was a miracle he'd been extracted alive, albeit barely, from the mangled wreckage. The other driver apparently had some minor injuries. There were no further details in the relatively brief report to explain why he'd failed to stop at the stop sign besides saying he'd passed a sobriety test on the scene.

Next, he called Donald Rasmussen, an old acquaintance who had a solo practice that subsisted primarily on personal injury cases. Donald was in the sunset of his career—nearly sixty-five years old, with a shock of white hair that was conspicuously sparse at the very top of his head. He was considerably overweight, with a belly that would have easily blended in among its kindred in a maternity ward. He had an irrepressible obsession with short-sleeved dress shirts, which when combined with a mismatched tie and suspenders, seemed to indicate his choice of raiment was solely for his own pleasure and not for his beholders. Yet there was something about Donald that endeared him to colleagues, something unfamiliar and out of step with the times; for when he handled a case, he seemed far less interested in making money than in establishing the truth and doing the right thing.

"How are you, young man?" he bellowed amicably as he picked up the receiver in his office.

Tim smiled at the familiar greeting and began to explain the nature of his request.

"I'd be glad to see what I can find," Donald assured him. "Would it be okay for me to visit the young man myself and talk to him, before I start looking around and poking my nose into other people's business?"

"Ah . . . sure, that would be fine. And give me a call if you run into any problems."

"I sure will. How's the good judge anyway? Is he talking of retirement yet?"

"Not that I've heard."

"Well, I don't know how much longer I can keep this up. It seems harder to get out of bed in the morning with each passing day. I'm getting too old for this. In any case, I'll get back to you in a couple of weeks—how does that sound?"

"That sounds good, Don. Thank you."

〜〜〜

When he reviewed the police report, Donald discovered that the other driver didn't have insurance at the time of the accident. This would likely be a major stumbling block in the way of receiving compensation for the injuries sustained. He had dispatched a letter to the person in question and was surprised on Friday a week later when his receptionist announced that a Mr. Pablo Pérez was waiting to see him.

He rose from his desk and went out into the reception area, where there were two men in their late twenties or early thirties waiting to see him.

"Good afternoon, gentlemen. I'm Donald Rasmussen, nice to meet you," he said, as he greeted each of them warmly with a handshake.

"I am Paco, and this is Pablo. I'm his cousin—his English not so good, so I come to help him."

"Oh, I see. Well, come on into my office and I'll tell you what this is about."

The cousins sat down, looking around the office and glancing nervously at each other, as they waited for the attorney to retrieve a document from a stack of folders on his bookshelf.

"So," Donald began, "the reason I reached out to you is because I'm representing the individual who was in the car your cousin drove into. That individual was very badly injured. He is still fighting for his life as we speak."

A grave look came over Paco's face, as he turned to his

cousin and in a torrent of Spanish explained to him what had been said. Pablo's eyes widened in horror and his breathing became audible. He said something to Paco, who then turned to Donald.

"He will die?"

Donald's brow furrowed, then he shook his head. "I don't know. He *could* die . . ."

Pablo seemed to understand what he had said, and he hastily made the sign of the cross and glanced upwards, whispering something that might have been a prayer. Then he turned to Paco and said something—to which Paco replied—and there was another brief back and forth between them until Paco finally turned to Donald and said, "He says judge already said it was okay."

"What judge?"

"After the accident, he go to court, and when judge finish he told him to go and see his doctor for treatment."

Donald was puzzled. "His doctor? Hmm . . . if you don't mind, I'd like to get in touch with his doctor and get Pablo's medical records from him."

"Sure. Here is doctor's card. He will tell you everything," Paco said, looking relieved.

At this point, Donald had a pretty good idea about the prospects of a financially viable lawsuit against the young man seated across from him.

"So, he is very sick? The other person?" Paco asked at Pablo's urging.

Donald nodded.

Pablo fumbled in his pockets and began to cobble together an assortment of crumpled bills—a twenty-dollar bill and six or seven others that all appeared to be one-dollar bills. Paco said something that sounded like it was meant to discourage him. Pablo hesitated for a second, then shook his head and defiantly placed the untidy cluster of bills on the table.

Donald thought he understood, but was at once amused and flabbergasted. He had never before been in a situation like this one.

"He says he feels very sad for the man who was hurt," Paco said, cringing with embarrassment. "He wants to give him this money because maybe it can help him."

"Oh, I'm sorry, but I can't take the money," Donald said, sounding genuinely apologetic. "But I'll be sure to tell him that you wish for him to get better," he added awkwardly, his face turning beet red.

Paco scooped up the bills and handed them to Pablo, explaining what had just been said. Pablo reluctantly took them back and started stuffing them in his pockets. He turned to Donald.

"Not enough?" he said in broken English. "I bring some more. I try to help. I'm sorry."

"Thank you, Pablo," rejoined Donald, "you're a good man."

As he escorted them out, he gave his receptionist Pablo's doctor's business card and instructed her to contact his office for his medical records. He again reflected on the fact that of all his encounters with defendants, this would have to rank as the strangest. An unexpected phone call from Pablo's doctor two days later only compounded his bemusement.

"Er . . . hello?" he began hesitantly as he picked up the receiver.

"My name is Dr. Miller, and I'm calling with regard to a request I received from your office for Mr. Pérez's medical records. We're sending them over, but I'd like to throw in my two cents on this matter since my patient has a limited ability to communicate in English."

"Sure, I appreciate the call. I met him a couple of days ago and he seemed like a nice guy."

"So, basically, Josué—or Pablo, as he is better known—has a rare condition called narcolepsy that developed about a year ago. Initially, we had a very tough time getting his tests approved by the insurance company. So, it's unfortunate that it took a motor vehicle accident and an order from a judge for them to finally approve the right testing and treatment. He's been doing great since he was put on the right medication for his condition."

"I remember he mentioned a judge when he was here, but I wasn't sure what he was talking about."

"Pablo received a citation for reckless driving as a result of the accident, and I had to provide records to the court showing he'd been trying to get medical help for his problem but had been refused it. He normally doesn't drive, but on that particular day he had to go into work, and his cousin who works at the same place and usually drives them both in, had to stay home. Pablo told me he drank two large cups of coffee in the morning so he would stay awake, but clearly that didn't work."

"You said his insurance company initially prevented him from getting the appropriate test. Would you happen to have their contact information?" Donald asked.

"I don't have it in front of me, but I'd be glad to have my assistant fax it over to you. Let me tell you, those insurance company people were pretty awful! I had a testy conversation with one of their doctors, who was in over his head and didn't even know it. And he started getting really cocky with me when I challenged his assessment of Pablo's condition. If you're looking for anyone to sue, that would be the person to go after."

Donald was listening very intently.

"Actually, Mr. Rasmussen, you know what, would you mind holding for a second. I think I might have written down the details of that conversation in Josué's chart. I might even have the name of the doctor. Hold on one second."

There followed the sound of quiet breathing with typing in the background, intermittently broken by Dr. Miller softly mumbling to himself as he clicked through his records.

"Yup, there it is! Friday, August 25th, two forty-five pm. I spoke to a Dr. William Young at Iatros Solutions—they're the outfit that decides who gets to live or die on behalf of the insurance company. Guy was a total schmuck! Normally I don't write that stuff down, but that day I was so hot under the collar that I made sure I wrote down every single detail, and I'm glad I did. If you're looking for a villain, that's your man—Dr. William Young."

Donald was dumbfounded and remained silent for a few more seconds. Then he thanked Dr. Miller for his time and hung up. As he shook his head in bewilderment, he called Tim Lacroix's cell phone number.

Chapter Seventeen

LAURA WAS AWAKENED by a phone call at about two thirty in the morning. It was her mother-in-law. "Laura? I'm sorry to wake you. It's Debbie, Will's mother. I'm so sorry to bother you but I got a call from the hospital . . ."

Laura scrambled to sit up as she fumbled to turn on the bedside lamp. "What . . . what's going on?" she asked, squinting reflexively as the bright light came on.

"I'm not sure why they called me first, but Will's had a major setback and they had to bring him by ambulance to the emergency room at Hampton Roads Medical Center. I'm getting ready to go in. Can you meet me there?"

"Sure," she said as her feet patted the ground back and forth, searching for her slippers; she eventually managed to get them on, albeit in reverse—with the left one on her right foot and vice versa. Shuffling into the bathroom, she hastily pulled on a pair of sweat pants and a well-worn fleece hoodie with the stubborn, barely legible remnants of the word CALIFORNIA stamped across its front. She knew it was ugly and shabby, but it always seemed to magically appear when she needed a jacket in a hurry, inexplicably managing to elude the periodic purges of clothing no longer deemed worthy enough to keep. Laura was about to turn out the light and exit the bathroom when she had second thoughts and decided to go back in and brush her teeth, staring vacantly into the mirror at her own bloodshot eyes as she passed the toothbrush aimlessly back and forth over her teeth.

The roads were clear and she was able to get to the ER in less than ten minutes. She found her mother-in-law in the waiting area.

"I was so sorry to wake you, Laura, but the hospital called and said we needed to come in right away," she said. "Bill's away in Missouri at a meeting."

The two women approached the receptionist whose gaze was focused intently on the clock on the opposite wall, as if she could use her powers of concentration to coax the minute hand to hurry along its path and bring the night shift to an end.

"We're here to see William Young," Mrs. Young said.

The receptionist seemed startled at first by their presence, then grabbed her computer mouse and jiggled it to reactivate her dormant screen. "Wha . . . what was the name again?" she asked, clearing her throat.

"William Young."

"Thank you. Let's see . . . oh, there he is! He's in C4, one of the critical rooms. Let me call his nurse and make sure it's okay for you all to go back there." She clicked on the computer screen and began conversing softly with someone through her earpiece. Then, with the call completed, she told them that someone would be coming out shortly to meet to them.

Barely two minutes later, a stocky man in hospital scrubs with unruly graying hair and an impeccable set of white teeth appeared. He introduced himself as Dr. Turner Riddick. His voice was deep and mellow.

"Who is everyone here?" he asked as he led them into an empty conference room. "Oh, I didn't realize there was a wife," he remarked after Laura introduced herself. "In his contact information for his next-of-kin he listed Mrs. Debbie Young. That's why we called you first," he said, addressing Will's mother.

The two women exchanged awkward glances but said nothing.

"So, William was brought in urgently from the skilled nursing facility because his blood pressure became dangerously low," Dr. Riddick explained. "It appears that he may have a condition called sepsis, which is when an infection becomes so severe that it starts to cause many of his organs—like his heart, lungs, brain and kidneys—to malfunction. We've started him on antibiotics, as well as medications to keep his blood pressure within a normal range. Given how sick he is, we also had to put him back on the ventilator through his tracheostomy, at least for the next twenty-four hours or so, while we get the sepsis under control. I understand he'd been able to remain off the ventilator for several days prior to coming in, and that there were even plans underway to remove the tracheostomy tube.

Obviously that plan has been shelved given the turn of events. He is very sick—very, very sick, you need to know that. The next twenty-four to forty-eight hours are going to be crucial, in that there is a real possibility William may not survive this."

He paused to let the information sink in. Laura could see her mother-in-law's eyes beginning to glisten, but there was a streak of quiet defiance in her facial expression.

"Do either of you have any questions?" Dr. Riddick said.

There was silence.

"Okay, well, I have one question," he added. "I'm not sure who should answer this, but I'm going to spit it out anyway. Normally, it's the spouse who makes decisions on the patient's behalf. Since he listed you," indicating Debbie, "as his next-of-kin, is there anything else I need to know regarding who to contact for important updates and decisions?" Turning to Laura, he asked, "Are you legally married, separated or divorced?"

"She's still very much his wife," Mrs. Young replied. "We're going to make decisions together."

"Alright, that's helpful. One more question."

The two women looked at him anxiously, knowing what was coming.

"Do you think he would want us to resuscitate him if, in his current state, his heart stopped beating unexpectedly?"

"That's a difficult question to answer, Dr. Riddick. Unfortunately, we haven't discussed that particular issue. So, I'd say give it a try in case it's something easily reversible, and if that doesn't work let him go. Would you agree, Laura?"

Laura hesitated briefly, then nodded.

"I think that's reasonable," Dr. Riddick observed. "It's difficult for anyone to anticipate every situation and know what they want in advance. Well," he said, as he prepared to leave, "that's all I have for right now. I'm happy to walk back there with you so you can see him. He'll be moved to intensive care once they have a bed available, and the ICU team will give you further updates. But if anything changes while he's still down here, I'll be sure to let you know."

Being back in the hospital after several months away felt at once disappointing and familiar to Laura. And for some strange reason, the familiarity was reassuring since she didn't feel stressed and overwhelmed like she had before. She wondered whether it was because this was the second time around, or whether it was because the state of her relationship with Will had changed.

Despite having only a few interactions with her in-laws, except when they ran into each other at St. Matthew's, Laura was starting to feel comfortably close to Mrs. Young. When Dr. Riddick had asked them about whether or not Will would have wanted to be resuscitated, her mind had flashed back to the day he'd angrily berated her for not letting him die following the accident. She decided not to bring this up now, so as not to complicate the situation, especially because it was unclear whether what he'd said during that bitter exchange counted as a rational decision. The fact that he'd designated his mother—not her—as his next-of-kin was a stunning revelation although not entirely unexpected. It meant that he wanted nothing to do with her. So, she decided she would keep up appearances for the sake of her in-laws while taking the backseat when any decisions came up.

Judge Young returned two days later from his meeting, and he was eager to visit his son at the hospital as soon as possible. On that same day, as it happened, Laura was already there, seated at Will's bedside. Her face brightened considerably when she saw her in-laws enter the room.

"I . . . er . . . I just want to say thank you," Laura said, blushing, as they exchanged greetings.

Her in-laws smiled at her. "Don't mention it, Laura. It was our pleasure to help," Judge Young replied.

A few weeks before, Laura had awakened in a panic when she realized that she'd missed the second payment on Will's car. She'd tossed and turned the rest of the night, trying to remember where she'd put the invoice. That morning, before heading out to work, she sorted through a pile of statements and unpaid bills but couldn't find it. At the first given opportunity—during recess—she called the financing department of the car dealership, who referred her to the bank that had issued the loan.

After being placed on hold for a couple of minutes, a woman came on the line and asked what kind of assistance she needed. Laura gave her the account number and the woman looked it up. "It was paid in full about two weeks ago," she said brusquely, "the balance is zero dollars. Anything else I can help you with?"

Laura's heart skipped a beat. "Oh, I didn't realize the entire balance had been paid," she ventured hesitantly.

"Yes ma'am, your husband sent in a cashier's check for the entire balance."

"My husband?" Laura asked, confused. "Are you sure?"

"There's a cashier's check from a Mr. William V. Young for the balance of the amount outstanding. Isn't that your husband?"

"Oh, that's my father-in-law. I didn't know he was planning to do that."

"Well, he did, so you won't be hearing from us anymore. Is there anything else I can do for you today, Mrs. Young?"

"No, and thank you very much."

Laura had picked up the phone several times afterwards and almost dialed her father-in-law's number, but chickened out at the last minute, coming up with a plausible excuse each time why it wasn't the right time to call. Then, when she finally received the payout from the insurance company for the totaled vehicle, the situation felt more awkward and urgent than ever. Was she supposed to give him the money from the payout in return? It was less than the balance of the loan, but it still made sense that she should turn it over to him.

Finally, one Saturday afternoon, she steeled herself and dialed her father-in-law's number, while wondering how she could gracefully broach the topic.

"Hello, Laura," he said, identifying her from the caller ID.

She meandered around the subject at first, but finally managed to disclose the reason she'd called. When she'd finished explaining, he uttered the words that were music to her ears.

"No, you don't owe us anything. Debbie and I were happy to help. Consider it a late wedding gift from us—not very flashy, I admit, but practical nonetheless," he chuckled.

Recollecting the exchange, Laura thought it was tinged with more than a little irony, since the belated wedding gift arrived at a moment in time when there wasn't much of a marriage left.

♒

After Judge Young paid his first visit to Will at the hospital, Laura and her in-laws arranged to meet there on the following day. As the trio made their way into the intensive care unit, they ran into Dr. Salim, one of the trainee doctors overseeing his care. He was a bespectacled individual in his mid-thirties, tall and gawky, with a kind engaging demeanor, and the impressive ability to remember people's names after only one meeting. Most people were thrown off-balance when he addressed them by name the second time they saw him, and many found themselves casting urgent, surreptitious glances at his name tag so as to memorize his.

"I don't know what this means in terms of the big picture, but Will is off pressors today," he remarked noncommittally.

"Off what?" Mrs. Young asked.

"Off the medications we were using to maintain his blood pressure in the normal range."

"That's good news, right?" she said, hopefully.

"It might be. Time will tell. He's better today than when he came in, although he's not out of the woods yet. Anything could change at any time," Dr. Salim admonished.

"And he's still off the ventilator?" This from Judge Young.

"Yes, and we've been leaving his speaking valve on during the day in case he wakes up and wants to say something."

"Is he still delirious?" the judge asked.

"When I saw him about five this morning, he was still sleepy and out of it. But then most people are like that if you wake them up that early and try to have a conversation with them. We'll get a better sense of how he's doing as the day wears on."

They thanked Dr. Salim, who was already inching away from them with a polite smile on his face, barely disguising the fact he was eager to be elsewhere.

Nell, Will's day nurse, was there again today. She'd taken care of him on the previous day, when Laura had caught her mother-in-law rolling her eyes and letting out a sigh as they listened to her stumbling through an implausible explanation for a medication change ordered by the doctors. She'd seemed inexperienced and easily frazzled, and as such inspired doubt and a sense of insecurity.

"Hello," Nell said mechanically—her face expressionless—when she greeted them. "When he woke up around six thirty this morning, he was asking for you," she said to Mrs. Young.

"He did?" Mrs. Young asked, her voice rising in surprise. "Was he still disoriented?"

"I don't know, I wasn't here."

The three exchanged bewildered glances, and Laura cringed inwardly.

"Well," Nell added, "that's what was passed along to me by the night nurse. I don't know any more than what I just told you." She paused briefly and then added, "I have to check William's vitals and make some adjustments to the equipment, so you'll need to move over there," indicating a corner of the room where there was a small cluster of chairs for visitors' use.

The trio moved cautiously, careful not to trip over any tubes or cables going to or from the bed to the various devices attached to Will. They seated themselves on the molded plastic chairs. The room was much smaller than the one at St. Matthew's, and the perpetually unopened blinds added to the existing aura of gloom.

Judge Young unfolded the newspaper he'd brought with him and began to read, while Laura and Mrs. Young conversed in low tones. Over the past couple days, their ritual consisted of sitting for an hour or two in the morning awaiting updates from the doctors, with possibly another visit later in the day. There'd been no interactions with Will so far.

About half an hour into the visit, the silence was broken by a loud voice coming from Will's bed, startling them all.

"Laura! Lauraaah!"

They all scrambled to their feet and gathered around the bed.

"I'm here, Will, I'm right here!" said Laura breathlessly, moving in close to where Will could see her.

"Let's go home! I want to go home!"

Nell came around from the foot of the bed, where she had

been typing her nursing notes on her mobile computer unit, and stood over Will on the opposite side of the bed from Laura. "Mr. Will, do you know where you are?"

"I'm in the hospital," he bellowed impatiently, "and I want to go home!"

"You can't go home yet. You still need to be in the hospital."

"I want to go home now!"

"No, Mr. Will, you can't go home—you're still very sick. If you try to leave the hospital now you will die!" Nell countered heatedly, her words and tone of voice causing Laura and her in-laws much consternation.

"I can go home whenever I want!" Will insisted.

"Well, in that case," she said belligerently, "I'm gonna get you the forms to sign saying you want to leave the hospital against medical . . ."

"Hold it right there, nurse!" Judge Young interrupted. "Please have the doctor come in to evaluate my son right now. I find your confrontational approach quite unhelpful!"

Nell's face flushed scarlet and she stormed out of the room. Mrs. Young, unsure of where she was going or what she intended to do, followed her out of the room and asked to speak to Yvonne, the nurse in charge. Yvonne came over and listened to her calmly, then agreed to summon Dr. Salim immediately.

As Mrs. Young came back into the room, she cracked a big smile and shook her head in mock disapproval at her husband, who was already feeling somewhat awkward and embarrassed about his unexpected outburst.

"What's the matter, Bill? Death Nell finally tripped you up? In all the years I've known you, I've never seen you go off the rails like that. Mmm . . . mmm . . . mmm . . . what a sight to behold! You sure told her!"

Judge Young shrugged self-consciously.

Laura suppressed a chuckle. "Death Nell?" she asked.

"Your father-in-law has a sneaky sense of humor—don't be fooled by appearances. From the minute he saw that girl yesterday, he knew she was going to be trouble. He was the one who gave her that nickname."

Dr. Salim and Yvonne came into the room a few minutes later.

"Hey, Will, I'm Dr. Salim. How are you feeling?"

"I'm fine, I want to go home."

"Well, I see you've made quite a bit of progress since earlier today. Tell me something—do you know where you are?"

"I'm at the hospital."

"And why are you here?"

"Because I'm sick . . ." replied Will, sounding mildly irritated.

"Um . . . er . . . okay, and what month is it?

"Today is December tenth, two thousand and fifteen."

Dr. Salim looked up at Yvonne, who smiled and observed that it was the eleventh and not the tenth.

"Wow, that's impressive! You're a day off, but it's still quite remarkable!"

"You need to update the whiteboard," Will said drily, shifting his gaze to the communication board on the wall directly in front of him.

"Aah, very clever! Yes, we will update the whiteboard. So, when you say you want to go home, do you mean your actual home, or back to the skilled nursing facility?"

"I want to go home."

Dr. Salim frowned briefly, but managed to regain his smile quickly.

"Okay, understood. Tell me, Will, do you recognize everyone here in the room?"

"That's my wife Laura, my mom and dad, you're Dr. Salim,

and I didn't get the name of the nurse who came in with you . . ."

"Yvonne."

"And the nurse who was here before is called Nell."

"Very good. Clearly, you're progressing a lot faster than we expected. We hadn't initiated any plan to send you directly home from the hospital, but we'll start looking into it right away. Let me speak to my attending physician and we'll get the case manager involved so we can figure out what arrangements we'll need to make to get you settled at home—like a motorized wheelchair, home nursing care and the like. It will probably take a few days to get everything in place, so you'll have to bear with us."

Will nodded.

"Very well, I'll be back with the rest of the rounding team later," said Dr. Salim, as he and Yvonne turned to go.

"Hi Laura—I'm so glad to see you," Will began, turning his head towards her, with an unfamiliar tender look in his eyes.

Chapter Eighteen

IT TOOK ABOUT ten more days to get everything arranged so Will could go home directly from the hospital; but he waited patiently, knowing that the process had been set in motion. Laura had prepared for this eventuality in some respects, like choosing a house with a large bedroom on the ground level, and without any steps leading up to the front porch. But when things became more acrimonious and unpredictable with Will, she'd dispensed with the notion of his coming home to live, and embarked on the process of fashioning an independent life for herself. Now she was terrified at the sudden turn of events, as she scrambled to prepare for his return.

Janice, Will's physical therapist at the hospital, was an excellent resource who never seemed to run short of practical ideas and suggestions to help with the process of resettling him. It was a personal mission for her, since she'd grown up with a mother who was quadriplegic. Indeed, the reason she'd decided to become a physical therapist in the first place was to help people like her mother. She exhaled positive energy and words of hope, carefully referring to Will's physical limitations as a "potentially disabling condition" rather than as a "disability."

Will had his tracheostomy tube removed a day or two after he left the intensive care unit. After this, he could speak freely without having to wait for the respiratory therapist to put his speaking valve on in the morning. Laura and her in-laws remained apprehensive that he might relapse into the dark state of mind he'd been in at St. Matthew's, but it never happened. The subject of divorce never came up again either.

Thursday was the big day—the day Will's wheelchair was being delivered to him in the hospital. From everything Janice had told them, it was the one thing that made all the difference between being bed-bound and totally dependent on others, and having a way of getting around that was a giant leap towards independence.

Will's parents were there, as were Laura and her mother. Janice came in too, even though she was officially off duty. She wore black jeans and an attractive purple wool sweater that matched her sneakers. Laura was so used to seeing her in uniform that she momentarily failed to recognize her when she first entered the room.

"Oh, hey Janice! It's so nice to see you!"

"You didn't think I was going to miss this, did you?" Janice replied, beaming.

A few minutes after nine, the technician from the medical equipment company arrived, pushing the power wheelchair, which appeared a lot bulkier than Laura had expected. With the help of Janice and Will's nurse, they hoisted him into the wheelchair and strapped him in.

"Alright," began Mark, the technician, addressing Will, "I'll start by giving you an introduction to how this works. There'll be a lot to learn over time, but for today I want to focus on the basics of how to get safely from point A to B. This wheelchair has a combination control system with a 'sip and puff' controller, as well as a head array and a control panel with a virtual keyboard. You use the straw to navigate the control panel or to type on the keyboard. It also has some limited Bluetooth capabilities that may be used with a smartphone, but I'd like to emphasize that the key word there is 'limited.' After this demonstration, I'll leave you the manual. And I'll stop back tomorrow before you leave the hospital to make sure you're comfortable. We normally do a follow-up home visit after about a week."

Besides Janice, no one else knew what he was talking about; but there were "oohs" and "aahs" when he started the demonstration.

"See this straw over here? That's kind of like a joystick. Go ahead and blow nice and strong into the straw and let's see what happens. I'm gonna get out of the way here."

"And you don't have to keep blowing once it starts moving," Janice chimed in.

Will blew into the straw and the wheelchair started to move forward.

"Okay, suck into the straw," Mark said.

He sucked some air and the wheelchair stopped.

"Alright, so blow to move forward and suck to stop. What do you think would happen if you sucked in right now from a standstill position? I don't want you to do it because there are people behind you, but tell me what you think would happen."

"I'd go backwards?"

"Yup, that's right. And if you were going backwards how do you stop?"

"By blowing."

"There you go! As simple as that. That's where the 'sip and puff' comes from, or 'suck and blow' if you will. Now let's take it to the next level. I'm gonna show you how to use the controls on the headrest and then the keyboard. There's tons of things you can do with this toy, but just like anything else it will take some time to figure it out and get comfortable with it."

As Mark demonstrated the features, with Janice challenging him with questions that only the two of them seemed to comprehend, the others smiled and shook their heads in amazement.

Judge Young was mesmerized. "In all my life, Debbie," he whispered, "this is the closest thing I've ever seen to magic! If I hadn't been here myself, I would never have believed it."

When the initial orientation was over, Mark told Will they'd be leaving the room to take the wheelchair on a test drive down the hallway. Will's face lit up with excitement.

"Alright, let me open both doors to give you enough room to get out. And remember, go slow until you get comfortable. Lean right on the headframe to turn right and left to turn left, and tilt your head back if you want to do a hundred-and-eighty-degree turn. I'll walk alongside you in case you need help."

As soon as the doors were opened, Will had the straw in his mouth and the wheelchair eased out noiselessly through the doorway and turned right. Janice walked briskly alongside Mark as they followed Will. At the end of the hall, the trio made a left turn and disappeared from view, reappearing five minutes later. Will had a triumphant grin on his face, while Janice brushed tears of joy from her eyes. Even Mark bore a satisfied smile on his face.

"He's a pro!" he exclaimed. "I've done at least a hundred quad chair starts in my career and he's by far my easiest! He figured out the basic controls in no time. Strong work, man!"

Will cruised slowly past Laura and his parents as he reentered the room, before carefully maneuvering the wheelchair into a complete about-turn and coming to a stop close to where he'd started.

"Excellent! We'll do another run tomorrow before you leave the hospital to make sure you're comfortable. Unfortunately, they're not gonna let you drive around between now and tomorrow—you know, all that liability stuff. But once you're home, you'll have lots of time to play with your new set of wheels. Any questions before I leave?"

"You were going to show me . . ." Will hesitated.

"Yes sir, I didn't forget. Let's do it right now. Where's your phone?"

Until this moment, it hadn't occurred to Will that he no longer had a cell phone. His had been destroyed in the accident and he hadn't needed one since. He looked up at Laura, who fumbled in her jacket pocket and produced hers.

"So," Mark said, "we'll program hers today and we can switch to yours when you get one." He placed her phone on the console and began typing on the keyboard. "Obviously, you won't need to do this. It's just for the initial setup."

Once he'd completed the task, he stood back and explained how it worked. "Alright, done. There's a microphone and speaker embedded on your headpiece to the left. Whenever you want to make a phone call just say 'Call,' followed by the name of whoever it is you wish to call or the ten-digit number, and the number or contact will show up on your phone. It will ask you to confirm before dialing. Once you're done with the phone call say 'End,' and it will disconnect. Are you ready to make your first phone call?"

Will looked around briefly, pondering who to call, until the corners of his mouth lifted in a smile. "Call Duncan Young!" he said loudly into the microphone.

Chapter Nineteen

IN ANTICIPATION OF Will's discharge from the hospital, Laura had taken some time off from work preceding the two-week winter break so she'd have ample time to adjust to the transition. Yet the days seemed to fly by in one frenetic blur. There were people coming in and out of the house every day: Will's parents, Laura's mother, a nurse, a physical therapist and an occupational therapist from the home healthcare agency. By the time their day came to an end, they were both wiped out, and found themselves looking forward to the end of the week when the pace slowed down.

Christmas Day was memorable for the blissful experience of waking up with nowhere to go and nothing to do. It was one of the few days they'd had so far when they could engage in casual, meandering conversation—something they hadn't done in a long time, probably not since the early years of their marriage.

Transferring from the bed to the wheelchair took a lot of practice, and she and Will were just beginning to advance beyond a clumsy ritual of fumbling and grunting that on a few occasions ended with a loud thud as they both toppled onto the floor. They'd practiced the routine a number of times with each of the physical therapists, including Janice. Like any skill, it always seemed a lot easier to accomplish when the person doing it had done it several times before. And even though the slide and spin boards that had been provided to help with the transfer were supposed to facilitate the process, learning to use them optimally was an art form in itself.

Will was receiving nourishment through a feeding tube implanted in his stomach because he still had trouble swallowing. Laura attached a plastic bottle of artificial nutrients to the tube three times a day. He didn't really miss the taste of food, which he'd been told he might. His speech therapist at the hospital suggested that the tracheostomy may have been interfering with his swallowing; and now that it was out, she'd scheduled him for an evaluation in the second week of January.

The challenge of learning so many new skills left little room for self-deprecation and dark brooding. Will seemed to have come alive with curious energy, eager to master the controls of his wheelchair. And he was looking forward to starting his sessions at the Seven Pines spinal rehab facility, which wasn't too far from where they lived, and which came highly recommended by Janice.

"It's a shame that nobody told us about that rehab before Janice happened to mention it," Will told Laura one day.

"It is. It's probably because when they moved you over to the skilled nursing facility you were still comatose and they didn't think you'd wake up. So the spinal injury issues were put on the back burner."

"Well, they should have thought about it when I started to get better. I hope I haven't lost ground because of the delay. If I hadn't gotten sick and gone back to the hospital, I'd still be languishing at St. Matthew's. You saw how long they dithered with the tracheostomy? It probably could have come out weeks ago."

"Didn't they have physical therapists there who worked with you daily?" Laura asked timidly.

"First and foremost, they didn't even see me daily—they only came in two to three times a week. Secondly, all they did was passive exercises, like bending my arms and legs, nothing more."

Laura remained silent. She still trod gingerly whenever the conversation touched on Will's time at St. Matthew's, afraid she might accidentally trigger a reappearance of that foul-tempered, capricious version of her husband—the one who'd vanished since the night he'd been rushed to the ER. Along with this recollection, she reflected somewhat ironically on how their relationship had become the best it had been in a very long while despite all the new challenges. Whenever she leaned forward and put her arms around Will to pivot him in or out of his wheelchair—her knees locked against his to prevent him from sliding, his warm breath blowing against her neck—she felt an unexpectedly strong sense of intimacy and tenderness different from anything she'd experienced with him before.

〜〜〜

Coordinating Will's trips to the Seven Pines facility with Laura's work schedule presented them with yet another new challenge. His sessions would last about an hour to an hour-and-a-half, and the facility was a forty-five-minute drive away in the opposite direction from the school. So it would be difficult for Laura to drop him off there in the morning before work; even if she managed to do that, his session would be over by mid-morning, during school hours when she was teaching, and therefore not able to pick him up. He still wasn't ready to be left alone in the house. She briefly considered asking either her mother or her in-laws to see if they would be available to help with his care, but decided that the extent of his needs would be too much for them to handle. After tossing the dilemma around in her head for a couple of days, she brought it up to Will one morning as they waited for the home health care nurse to arrive.

"You might have to come to school with me for the first few weeks after I'm back at work. It would only be until we figure out a schedule for you during the day."

Will looked confused. "What would I do there all day?"

"Well, you'd be a kind of classroom volunteer. I discussed the idea with Dr. Sinclair, the principal, and she said it would be okay. You'd help the kids with sight words and reading—stuff like that."

"Stuff like what? What else would I be able to do? I can't walk, I can't lift anything, I can't play with them at recess, and I certainly do not want to be surrounded by a bunch of snotty third-graders wanting to know what happened to me. No thanks, I'll take a pass."

Laura sighed. "Will, I know this is difficult, but hear me out . . ."

"What about getting a private nurse to come in for the day when you're not around?"

"That's twenty bucks an hour for about ten hours a day, which comes to a thousand dollars a week that we don't have. I already thought of that."

Will's eyes narrowed and his jaw hardened.

"We don't have the money, Will. I don't make that much money."

"Couldn't you take more time off, just until I've gotten more comfortable around the house?"

"I might be able to get an additional week or two, but beyond that it would be unpaid time off, which we can't really afford; and I need to keep working to keep the healthcare insurance coverage going for you."

"Why don't I stay at my parents' house while you're at school?"

Laura shook her head. "Your parents are getting older. There's a lot of things they wouldn't be able to do for you. I think that's asking too much from them."

Will went silent and looked disconcerted.

"Will?" Laura said.

"Huh?"

Just then, the doorbell rang. It was Maureen, the nurse they were expecting. She was a petite woman in her mid-sixties, with steel-wool gray hair she wore in a bun. Of the three or four visiting nurses who took care of Will, she was the one who came most often. Her visits usually lasted exactly an hour, never more, never less, and she carried out her tasks in a perfunctory manner, with an insincere smile securely fastened onto her face.

Sometimes she would ask Will a question about how he felt or whether he had a certain symptom. But she never waited for his answer since she was apparently impervious to whatever he had to say—she simply moved on to a different topic. Laura had found this odd, and even wondered whether the woman might not be deaf. And invariably—at the end of every visit—she would step back, hold out her arms and announce enthusiastically to Will, "Looks like you're doing great! Keep up the good work, and I'll see you next time!"

After Maureen left, Laura had hoped to resume her conversation with Will regarding her return to work. But the physical therapist, Frank, appeared at the door as they opened it to see the nurse out. A couple of hours later, when they found themselves alone again, Will seemed a little more open-minded about finding a solution that took her needs as well as his into account.

"What if you left me at home in the morning, dropped me off at rehab during your lunch break, and then picked me up from there after work?"

She shook her head. "I spoke with Lori, the manager at Seven Pines. Their policy stipulates that patients are allowed to wait at the facility for an hour before their session and an hour afterwards. Beyond those limits, they cannot take responsibility for your care and well-being."

"What if I just stayed home by myself? After all, I'll have the home healthcare people coming in at intervals in the morning, so I won't be completely alone."

Laura exhaled deeply. "Will, that doesn't solve any of the problems—it doesn't get you to Seven Pines for the rehab you need, and it doesn't really solve the issue of who will take care of you while I'm at school because each of the home healthcare people comes in for a limited amount of time and focuses only on what they're there for. Also, once you start your sessions at Seven Pines, most of the home healthcare services, such as physical therapy and occupational therapy, will stop. We already talked about this—insurance will only pay for one, not both. Please work with me here."

"Are there any daytime care facilities I could go to? Like where you could drop me off and then pick me up after school?" Will suggested hopefully.

"None that I know of; and if they did exist, the insurance

issues would be the same—they wouldn't be covered."

"I hate insurance!" Will growled. "Why does this have to be so complicated?"

Laura was about to say something in reply, but changed her mind when she decided it was best to let the subject drop since they weren't getting anywhere. In the days that followed, they again considered different options, but these came to naught when they got to the part that involved someone other than Laura caring for Will at no additional cost. By the time school reopened, they still hadn't found a better solution, so Will resigned himself to capitulating to Laura's original plan.

They arrived in school early in the morning, about an hour before the students. By the time they started trickling into the classroom, Will had taken up his station at the back of the room, where he felt he would be the least conspicuous and most out of the way. He couldn't understand why his heart was pounding like it was since, as he told himself repeatedly, "They're just a bunch of third-graders—there's no need to be nervous"—but the words rang hollow. As they came in one by one, there would be a quick glance in his direction, followed by a double take, then occasionally a smile or a wave, followed by, in some cases, an exchange of hushed whispers.

Once they were all seated, and after Laura took roll call, she made an announcement. "Good morning, everyone. I hope you all enjoyed your winter break. I know you're wondering who our visitor is, so I'll go ahead now and introduce him. He is my husband, and you can call him Mr. Will. He'll be helping out, like the other parent volunteers we've had from time to time, with your sight words and reading. One thing that's different about him is that, because he was injured in a car accident, he's not able to move his arms and legs, so he needs a special wheelchair to get around."

A hand immediately shot up in the front row.

"Yes, Rosie, did you have something to say?" Laura said hesitantly.

"My big brother has a wheelchair just like that."

"Really?"

"Uh huh."

"How long has he had it?"

"Since before I was born. My mom said he was diving in the pool and broke his neck. He can do some pretty cool tricks with his wheelchair, like spinning . . ."

Just then the principal's voice came over the intercom for the daily announcements and pledge of allegiance, so Rosie never got to complete her story. But the little she had said made all the difference to Will, who was now feeling a lot more relaxed. Throughout the morning lessons, he grinned and nodded in acknowledgment at the children who turned around to smile or wave at him.

When it was time for their thirty-minute recess, the children lined up to leave the classroom and head outside. But as one boy started to approach Will instead, Laura intercepted him and instructed him to rejoin his classmates. A sullen expression formed on his face as he turned around and reluctantly went to the end of the line. As the line moved into the hallway, Laura signaled to Will, who set his wheelchair in motion and began navigating his way to the door, much to the fascination of the kids toward the end of the line who were near enough to watch. Once they were outside, the kids scattered, with some running in different directions and hollering excitedly, while others made a beeline for the jungle gyms and swing sets. The weather was especially nice for January, about fifty degrees without the chilly wind gusts, and the sky was clear. Laura left Will to intervene in an altercation that was brewing over who had the first claim to the swings; and as soon as she was a fair distance from him, the boy reappeared at Will's side. He'd clearly been waiting for an opportunity.

He had cold unsmiling eyes and the hard expression of someone to whom life had not been particularly kind. "I'm Elias," he said bluntly.

"Nice to meet you, Elias," Will said, looking over at where Laura stood, her back to him.

For what seemed like an eternity, Elias just stood there, staring at Will. Until he said, "How do you pee?"

"Um . . . excuse me?" Will said, trying very hard not to look flabbergasted and buying time to think through an appropriate reply.

"I mean, since you're not able to walk to the bathroom, how do you go?" Elias explained.

"Well . . . er . . . I have a tube called a catheter. When I go, the urine drains into a bag that's tied to my leg."

Elias had a puzzled expression on his face. "What's *u-ren?*"

"Oh, that's just a fancy grown-up word for pee-pee," Will said with a chuckle. "But, you know, it's one of those things you have to be careful not to talk about too much in public because it's not considered polite."

The boy cocked his head back, tilting it slightly to the left, something he did reflexively when he either doubted something or it didn't make sense to him. "Like now?"

"No, you're fine right now."

"Do you think . . . er, could I . . . um, could I see the bag?"

Will jerked his chin towards his right knee.

"If you lift up my pant leg just a little, you'll see it."

Elias cautiously raised the bottom of Will's sweat pants to reveal a clear, plastic bag about a quarter-way full of gold-colored liquid.

"Wow, awesome! I wish I had one like that!" the boy said excitedly. "But what if the bag gets busted?"

Will didn't get a chance to answer. Thirty seconds ago, Laura had turned and seen Elias talking to Will, and was immediately seized with a sense of dread, believing the boy was up to no good. As she started approaching, she'd seen Elias crouch down and reach for Will's urine bag, and she was convinced he was either trying to put a hole in it or open the drainage cap. She arrived after a panicked half-run, heaving with exertion, her face beet-red.

"What's going on here?" she asked tersely, unable to altogether suppress her anxiety.

Elias rose from the ground and stepped away from Will. There was that familiar baleful expression on his face. Although he was only half Laura's height, he looked menacing, like a cornered bobcat preparing to claw and bite its way out of a corner.

"Oh, nothing really," Will replied calmly, breaking the tension. "My new friend Elias and I were just chatting about urine bags—you know, just normal conversation. Elias is very curious—maybe he'll become a scientist one day, right Elias?"

A broad grin came over the boy's face. He nodded enthusiastically.

"I'm very pleased to hear that, Elias!" Laura said delightedly. "I'm glad to hear you've become a friend of Mr. Will's."

"It's nice to meet you, Mr. Will . . ." said Elias, before he went off to join the other kids.

"It was very nice to meet you too, Elias," Will said with a warm smile.

Chapter Twenty

WHATEVER IT WAS that drew Elias to Will was a mystery. But one thing that was not in doubt was the change in his behavior after Will had appeared on the scene, to the amazement of Laura, Dr. Sinclair and all the other teachers. He was no longer getting into trouble for shoving, pinching or pulling hair, or for profane outbursts. He seemed happy. At lunch or recess, he was always at Will's side, rushing to clear the way for his wheelchair or to pick up something that had fallen to the ground.

"Maybe Elias sees Dr. Young as a father figure," Dr. Sinclair suggested, as she and Laura discussed the sudden improvement in the boy's behavior. She was probably the only person in the school who referred to Will as Dr. Young. To everyone else, he was either Mr. Will or the man in a wheelchair.

The presence of a father—or the lack of one—had never come up during any of the turbulent incidents involving Elias at the school. After one or two meetings with the fiery Ms. Mundy, and being at the receiving end of her blistering magma of rage and invective, there was no room left to even consider the possibility of there being another parent. And the more Laura thought about Dr. Sinclair's theory, the more she felt there was some truth in it.

If she had any doubts in her mind, they were dispelled when the "Donuts with Dad" breakfast took place. It was an opportunity for each child to come to school with a father figure in their life, to share a simple breakfast of donuts. The previous year, Elias had brought his grandfather, whom he and his mother lived with. His grandfather was a soft-spoken eighty-something-year-old army veteran who suffered from emphysema, and carried a portable oxygen device with him, with the skinny plastic tubes looped over his ears and into his nostrils. The oxygen made a hissing noise whenever he inhaled, making him sound as if he was constantly sniffling. He walked with a large wooden cane and was rather hard of hearing. The old gentleman had been to the school a few times before for social activities, but never together with his daughter. She only came in when there was a crisis, which she usually succeeded in making a lot worse by the time she left.

When Elias invited Will to the donut breakfast, Will was unsure about what he should do. So he decided to discuss the matter with Laura during the lunch break that day.

"That's odd!" she said, looking bewildered. "Isn't his grandad coming this year?"

"I don't know anything about his grandad. I'm just telling you that he asked me."

"Well, let me look into it before you give him your answer," Laura said as she rose from her seat in the staff room, and went down the hallway to the dining hall where Ms. Mallory, the teaching assistant, had corralled the children. She returned after about five minutes.

"Well," she said with a shrug, "according to Elias, Grandpa Mundy hasn't been feeling well lately and won't be able to come. So you're free to accept the invitation—if you like."

On the day in question, Elias came running into the classroom as soon as he entered the school. He was meeting up with Will and Laura, since they'd agreed to meet there. The other children who were attending the breakfast went directly to the cafeteria, and would return to the classroom afterwards.

For various reasons, not everyone participated, although about three-quarters of them did. Some who were excluded were still looking forward to "Muffins with Mom," which took place a little later on in the year. Some children went to both, and some went to neither. So no one felt they were missing out, Laura always tried to come up with an interesting activity to fill up the half-hour or so taken up by the breakfast for those left behind.

There were a few bemused looks, mainly from the adults, when Will and Elias entered the cafeteria. Elias was gleeful and completely oblivious. He was even more delighted when Will offered him his donut. This generated some envious looks from his peers. One of the parents, a Mr. Ferguson, whose daughter, Felicia, was in a different class, came up to the table where Will and Elias were seated. He was a tall man with restless eyes and a large nose that in profile resembled an eagle's beak.

"Is that you, Elias?" he asked hesitantly.

Elias nodded, and the erstwhile gleeful expression on his face quickly faded away.

"Where's your granddaddy? I'd hoped to see him today."

"He wasn't feeling too good," Elias mumbled as his ears started turning red.

"Oh, I'm sorry to hear that. Tell him Mr. Ferguson said hello," he said, not once looking in Will's direction or acknowledging him in any way.

The exchange over, Mr. Ferguson returned to the table where his daughter Felicia was waiting. For a short while afterwards, Elias seemed subdued; but his ebullience quickly returned as he sank his teeth into his second donut, which was covered in white glaze and multicolored sprinkles. "Thank you for coming, Mr. Will," he said, as he contentedly munched away.

About ten minutes later, people began to leave and the students headed back towards their classrooms. As Will and Elias headed down the hall together, Will became thoughtful, reflecting on how everything seemed so familiar to him now. He'd been coming to the school for almost four weeks, and his initial apprehension about spending the day at an elementary school was a distant memory. He knew all of the children in Laura's class by name, and at least half of her fellow teachers.

His sessions were going well at the rehab facility as well. Laura usually drove him there immediately after school ended. It made for a gratifying—albeit grueling—end to a long day. The therapists were polite but relentless, and warned him that it might take some time before his body started to respond to the regular targeted exercises. By the time he and Laura got home after a full day of school followed by a rehab session, Will was exhausted and usually asleep by nine o'clock, while Laura often stayed up longer, preparing for the next day's lessons.

It was not clear what made Will remember Mr. Fogarty on one particular evening as they were heading home from Seven Pines.

"I miss old Mr. Fogarty!" he said, with a hint of wistfulness in his voice. "It's been a long while since the last time we saw him."

"Who? . . . Oh, you mean the old guy from the beach?"

"Uh huh."

"What made you think of him?"

"I don't know. His name just popped into my head."

Laura shrugged. "Well, maybe he's still dropping stones in the ocean like he's always done. How old is he now, do you think? He must be getting up there in years."

"I'd say probably in his late seventies, maybe even eighty, although he's always looked old to me, what with those shabby clothes, dilapidated hat and weather-beaten face."

"One of these days we should head out to the beach and see if he's still there," suggested Laura.

Will's eyes lit up. "How about this weekend?" he said enthusiastically.

She was a bit taken aback by his eagerness. "Um . . . well, actually I was thinking more towards summer. It's still February, so there'll probably be cold gusty winds down by the waterfront. And he probably doesn't go to the beach in the winter."

"No, he goes every day, even when it's snowing," Will insisted. "And I'm already excited by this idea. I think they're expecting sixty-two degrees on Saturday—that's not too bad if you dress right and stay out of the water."

Even in winter, temperatures varied a lot, so it was possible to go from twenty-two to seventy-two degrees in one day, or the other way around. Still, it was too early in the week to know if the weather prediction for Saturday would hold.

"Alright, if it's not too cold or rainy, we'll plan on going out there on Saturday," Laura said with a broad smile, having overcome her initial reluctance after seeing how much the prospect pleased Will.

Laura had purchased their van during the brief period of hectic preparation before Will left the hospital. It had belonged to the widow of a man who had died about six months earlier of complications from ALS. The former owner, still weary from her recently concluded emotionally exhausting journey, was eager to get rid of it and had sold it for the stunning bargain price of three thousand dollars. She would probably have paid Laura to take it off her hands had she shown even a hint of hesitation.

The vehicle was in excellent condition and had only sixty thousand miles on it. It came equipped with a side ramp that could be lowered onto the pavement, and the front passenger seat had been removed to make room for a power wheelchair. Once inside, Will just had to steer into place, after which Laura would lock the wheels and strap his seatbelt on. The van made it a lot easier for them to get around, since Laura didn't have to get Will in and out of his wheelchair whenever they drove somewhere.

Saturday arrived, and the weather seemed favorable to their outing. Will wanted to be there around three o'clock, since that was usually when Mr. Fogarty showed up. It was Will's first visit to the beach since before the accident. The parking garage was half-empty there at this time of year because the swimmers, surfers and sunbathers were absent, leaving the boardwalk to joggers, cyclists, walkers, and occasionally, people flying kites.

"VIP parking!" Will declared triumphantly as they pulled into one of the large parking spots.

Laura was amused. He'd been giddy with excitement since the

day they'd decided to come here.

They made their way out of the parking lot and crossed Atlantic Avenue at 17th Street, heading for the boardwalk. Even for this time of year, it was pretty deserted for a sunny Saturday afternoon, with only a handful of people strolling around in puffy jackets, who shivered and grimaced whenever a blast of wind blew off the ocean.

"It hasn't changed much since the last time we were here," Will mused aloud.

"No, it hasn't." Laura was concerned that coming to the boardwalk for the first time in a wheelchair might evoke some sadness or grief in Will. But on the contrary, he seemed happy to be there.

"What time is it?" he asked.

"About two forty-five," she replied, glancing at her watch. "He should be here soon."

The boardwalk—unlike what the name suggested—consisted of smooth concrete, and stretched three miles along the oceanfront. After turning right, they slowly made their way southward, with Laura strolling alongside Will's slowly moving powerchair. He'd become proficient at steering it, so she no longer hovered over him nervously, in anticipation of needing to grab him or power it off in case he veered dangerously out of control. Her gaze roamed the empty beach, where the breakers rippled across the face of the water, tumbling recklessly onto the wet sandy shoreline, sometimes sending an occasional seagull scrambling into the air as the water approached. The steady whoosh-whoosh of the waves as they rolled back and forth seemed somewhat muted unaccompanied by the familiar sound of squealing children running in and out of the ocean.

Five past three . . . Laura said nothing as she registered the time on her watch with a quick glance. They were still making their way towards the southern end of the boardwalk at a leisurely pace, and there was no sign of him yet. She debated whether she should propose turning back, then decided not to say anything. They were about half a mile from the end of the boardwalk.

"He's normally here by now," Will said suddenly, breaking the silence. His voice was a bit subdued.

"Oh, I'm sure he'll show up if it's his custom to be here every day. It's not as if he has to show up at exactly three o'clock on the dot."

Will was silent for a moment. "Let's start heading back. If he's not here by about three thirty then he's probably not coming. That would be way too late. And if he doesn't come, then I'll start to wonder if he's still alive, because he's never not shown up."

Laura felt her heart miss a beat. When Will mentioned Mr. Fogarty earlier in the week, that was the first thought that crossed her mind.

"Do you know where he lives? We can try to find him."

"I've no idea where he lives. He was always here at the beach. I don't even know if he has any family or friends."

By the time they got back to where they started, it was almost three thirty. Will was trying to put on a brave face, but she could see that he was not only disappointed but also worried about Mr. Fogarty's whereabouts. They were silent as they made their way into the parking lot, each keeping their disquieting ruminations to themselves. Up to this point, Laura hadn't invested any emotional energy in coming to the beach or finding Mr. Fogarty. She saw herself as no more than a facilitator. But now, suddenly, she found herself consumed by the desire to find out where he was and what had happened to him. She considered their options. Probably the best place to start would be to come back on a different day and ask a few of the local store owners and some of the runners who looked to be regulars if they'd seen him lately. If Will was up to it, they could come back on the following weekend if the weather was favorable. She even decided that if he didn't show any interest in the idea, she would still go on her own and ask around.

During the week that followed, Mr. Fogarty's absence dominated all their silent moments and unexpected nighttime awakenings. Will preferred to brood silently on the matter; once or twice when Laura tried to bring up the subject in conversation, he artfully redirected it to another topic as nonchalantly as possible. But he did offer a tepid endorsement of her proposal to return to the beach on the following weekend. She decided not to tell him of her plan to ask around if they were unsuccessful in this second quest for Mr. Fogarty, suspecting from his general lack of enthusiasm that he might try to pour cold water on her efforts.

Saturday arrived and this time it was much cooler, with a high of about fifty-two degrees at three o'clock. A cloud cover of gloomy gray blocked out the sun's radiance and was expected to last the entire weekend. But it was a lot less windy, so the air actually felt warmer than it had on the previous Saturday. This time around, they didn't venture far beyond the point where 17th Street met the boardwalk. Will didn't seem interested in doing anything more than sit in one spot and count the minutes. Once again, there was no sign of Mr. Fogarty. After a long wait, Will looked up at Laura.

"Three thirty-five," she announced wearily. She'd been planning to hold out till four if he didn't ask about the time.

"It's time to go," Will mumbled with an unmistakable tone of defeat in his voice. He gently jerked his head backwards and the powerchair spun around. As he leaned forward to blow into the straw to get the wheelchair moving, a raspy voice called out from the street, from the corner of a building about twenty yards ahead of them.

"Hey kid, is that you?"

Will and Laura both looked up in surprise, then a huge smile appeared on Will's face.

"Hey Mr. Fogarty, how are you doing? We were just starting to wonder what happened to you!"

He still wore his battered hat and the threadbare coat that was somewhere between jungle green and brown in color. Instead of the familiar knickerbocker pants and sandals, today he was clad in full-length pants and a pair of leather boots that were ashy gray for want of polish.

"What's with the chair?" he said, walking toward them.

Laura crinkled her nose when he was within smelling distance. He emitted an overpowering odor of seaweed mixed with stale sweat. As a broad grin stretched across his wrinkled brown face, Laura couldn't help but notice the unsightly array of blackened teeth and the numerous gaps between them. Underneath his wiry gray eyebrows, his brown eyes twinkled as he gazed at them.

"Oh, I had an accident and broke my neck," Will explained. "I can't move my arms and legs anymore, though I'm working at trying to get some of my strength back."

"That's a shame," Mr. Fogarty said, looking crestfallen, his smile gone. "I'm sorry to hear that."

Changing the subject, Will said, "This is my wife Laura."

"Ma'am," he said, addressing her with a polite nod.

"We came by last week and didn't see you," Laura said, with a warm smile. "We were starting to worry about you."

After hearing that, Mr. Fogarty appeared nervous and unsettled. "I put in too many rocks."

"You what?" Will said.

"Remember the rocks I put in the ocean to prevent the waters from receding?"

"Yes."

"Well, a couple of months ago, I was walking past the Keystone Motel, the one just down the road. It was about nine o'clock in the morning and they had the television on in the terrace. I saw they were talking about the oceans rising and how they figure that some of these buildings close to the shoreline might soon be under water. I think I went too far. I knew I should have stopped when I got to ten thousand."

Laura looked dumbstruck, but Will didn't miss a beat. "I don't think it's because of you, Mr. Fogarty. I think if it wasn't for you and your hard work, the shoreline would probably be half a mile out from where it is now. And since you're not putting in any more rocks, it shouldn't move any closer."

Mr. Fogarty's face wore an uneasy smile. "You really think so?"

"I know so. Everyone who lives here is happy about what

you did, so don't bother with what those know-nothing TV people from New York are saying. They don't even live here."

"Er . . . I think them TV folks was local people. They sounded real familiar with the streets and what goes on around here."

"But did you know that they're told what to say by the people in New York?"

"Oh, I see what you're saying," Mr. Fogarty said, sounding relieved. "And here I was, worried sick for two months that the rising sea level was all my fault! I'm sure glad I came around today and found you here."

"Me too," Will said, looking pleased.

"Well, I guess I better get going. So, do they think you'll ever walk again?"

Will shook his head. "Most likely not, but I'm okay with it now." After a brief pause, he said, "So, what do you do now that you're no longer taking care of the ocean?"

"I'm still taking care of it," he replied, "just not putting any more rocks into it. I still come over every day at high tide, just to keep an eye on things."

"Oh, so now you come in at high tide every day and not at three o'clock like you did before?"

"That'd be correct," Mr. Fogarty nodded.

A question flashed through Laura's mind, and by what he said next, Mr. Fogarty seemed to have read her mind.

"The doorman at Keystone saves me a copy of the newspaper every day—you know, the ones they give to the people that pay to sleep there. It has the tide chart predictions for every day, so I know when to come."

"That's good to know," Laura said. "Next time we're looking for you, we'll know to come at high tide."

After exchanging good-byes, Mr. Fogarty continued on his way to the beach, as Laura and Will headed to the parking lot.

"He's an interesting guy," Laura observed as soon as he was out of earshot. "And it seems like the two of you share quite a strong connection."

"I'll be the first to admit he's a little nutty, but he wakes up every day with a firm sense of purpose, which is more than you can say about a whole lot of people. You've got to admire that."

"That's true, I guess. How did he figure ten thousand rocks?"

"I was kind of surprised when he said that, but think about it: if he dropped a rock daily into the ocean for three hundred days, which is less than a year, then multiply that by thirty, you would have nine thousand rocks. If a year is three hundred and sixty-five days—not counting leap years—then it would come to less than thirty years. I know it's been more than twenty-five years since he's been doing this, so he's probably done the math. He's a little crazy, but also brilliant. Who else, besides fishermen and lifeguards would study the tide charts every day? And remember, this whole routine about dropping rocks in the ocean started when he noticed that temperatures in general were rising according to the *Farmers' Almanac*."

Laura smiled and shook her head incredulously as they got to the street and prepared to cross. Will was clearly very pleased about seeing Mr. Fogarty.

"You know one thing, Laura?" he said as they entered the crosswalk.

"What?"

"There's a whole bunch of people in this area—I mean, store owners, lifeguards, regular beachgoers—who count on Mr. Fogarty to show up and do his thing as a reminder to them that whatever they're going through is not as bad as it seems, and that life still goes on."

"Hmm . . . I see how that could be. It's certainly true for you—you look pretty stoked at having seen him! I guess someone should have mentioned that to Mr. Fogarty before he decided to change his regular schedule from three o'clock to high tide. He probably has no idea how many people base their sense of normalcy on his predictable routine," Laura remarked as they reached the van, and she started opening the rear sliding door on the passenger side.

Chapter Twenty-One

WHEN DOROTHEA MUNDY stormed into the school building that day at eleven fifteen, Agnes, the receptionist, knew trouble was brewing. As soon as she saw the diminutive silhouette appear at the main entrance and start stomping across the foyer, she scrambled out of her seat and bolted into Dr. Sinclair's office to warn her of the oncoming incursion. Normally, she was the one who called Ms. Mundy whenever she had to be summoned to discuss a disciplinary issue involving Elias; but Agnes knew she hadn't made any such call, which made the woman's sudden appearance all the more disquieting.

Agnes tapped once on the door and hurriedly pushed it open without waiting for a response to avoid being cornered in the hallway by the irate woman. Dr. Sinclair looked up from her work, and seeing the look in her receptionist's eyes, immediately surmised what was going on.

"Out there?" Dr. Sinclair whispered, as she briskly rose from her desk and tiptoed to the door that Agnes was forcefully holding shut. Putting her ear against the door panel, she listened for the sound of footsteps, but none came.

For the next two minutes, the two stood waiting silently by the door before exchanging bemused glances. After a brief nod from her boss, Agnes opened the door hesitantly, and peered into the hallway. The reception area was empty. Dr. Sinclair looked at Agnes skeptically, as if to express some doubt about whether Agnes had indeed seen Ms. Mundy.

Then came the shouting from the direction of Elias Mundy's classroom, and they knew the voice could have come only from one person.

"Go and get Mr. McDaniel, the security guard," the principal directed Agnes. "I need him to come quickly! It appears we have a situation in Mrs. Young's classroom." As Agnes scurried to find Mr. McDaniel, Dr. Sinclair braced herself and walked cautiously towards the commotion.

A sudden hush had fallen over the classroom when Ms. Mundy burst in, an array of curious, startled eyes all turning at once in her direction.

"Come here, Elias!" she barked.

Laura rose from her seat. "Hello, Ms. Mundy. What brings you here today?" she said, trying to sound calm and polite for the benefit of the children, despite inwardly feeling numb with terror.

"This is none of your business, so stay out of it! Elias, get over here right now!"

"Ms. Mundy . . ." Laura approached the enraged woman.

"I warned you before and I'm not going to warn you again.

You better stay out of this!" she commanded her once again.

Elias had risen to his feet and was fumbling to get his belongings together. From the look on his face, he appeared just as confused and frightened about his mother's behavior as everyone else.

"Hurry up, boy! I ain't gonna tell you but one more time before I start giving you a wuppin'!" she snarled impatiently.

Stuffing his books into his backpack, Elias maneuvered quickly between the desks and made his way to where his mother stood. When he was close enough to her, she grabbed his arm tightly causing him to wince with pain, but she didn't let go.

"So, is that your new daddy now?" she exploded, pointing directly at Will.

Will was seated in his usual spot in the corner of the room. He had been watching with growing consternation as the episode unfolded. His heart stopped when Dorothea Mundy's furious eyes met his.

"Go on, boy, tell me! Is that your daddy?" she screamed at her son, still keeping his arm in her vise-like grip.

"No."

"Then why in God's name did you go to the school breakfast with him instead of your granddaddy? And to think you would make up a story about your granddaddy being sick so that you didn't have to come with him! Why, Elias? Why would you do a rotten thing like that?"

Elias scowled and fixed his gaze on the floor. While he'd initially been frightened by his mother's sudden appearance, he now seemed to have adopted a defiant stance, which only fueled her anger more.

"Are you trying to take my child away from me?" she yelled, turning to Laura.

"No, Ms. Mundy . . ."

"Then why would you let my son go to a school activity with a total stranger without checking with me first?"

Laura groped around in her mind to come up with a response, while all the children looked aghast, and one or two started to cry. At that moment, the principal entered the classroom.

"Let's get out of here," Ms. Mundy yelled to her son, dragging him around her in a half-arc as she headed to the door, stopping briefly to turn towards Will. "And you stay away from my son, you crippled nigger!"

And with that she stormed off with Elias in tow, as shocked gasps and bewildered cries coursed through the classroom. Dr. Sinclair tried to stop her but she walked right past, deploying a barrage of invectives in her direction. Mr. McDaniel, who was right behind Dr. Sinclair, felt it prudent to step aside and let her pass.

It took a while to calm the children's distress. The principal's quiet, soothing manner was well-suited to this objective. And since the incident had occurred before lunch, forty-five minutes of outdoor recreation at lunchtime helped further restore a sense of normalcy. In addition, Dr. Sinclair arranged to have a substitute teacher help the teaching assistant watch the kids outside so that Laura could spend some private time with Will.

As they sat alone in the staff room, Will was silent. His expression was difficult to read.

"How are you doing?" asked Laura quietly.

"I'm fine. Better than Elias, anyhow," he replied mirthlessly.

"His mother is horrible. I'm so sorry about her!"

"No need to be. It wasn't your fault."

"That woman is a piece of work! Things were going so much better with Elias—it's such a pity. I don't know what Dr. Sinclair will or can do about a situation like this where the sole reason for a problem with a student is the parent. She can't penalize him for who is mother is. But she can't do nothing, because what's to stop Ms. Mundy from doing this again? And wait till the other parents hear from their kids what happened—we'll soon have a whole procession of them coming in here wanting to know what we're doing to keep their children safe from aggressive, foul-mouthed people like her. I don't envy Dr. Sinclair, that's for sure."

In the days that followed, Elias didn't come to school. Initially, it seemed logical and expected. But after a week went by and he still hadn't returned, the administrative staff became concerned. The incident had already been brought to the attention of the school board the day after it occurred, and there were ongoing discussions regarding the best course of action. A few phone calls were made to the contact numbers in Elias' records, but they weren't answered and the voicemail messages were ignored.

Finally, ten days after the episode, the school board sent a caseworker to Elias' grandfather's house, which was the only address on file. The caseworker was a burly man in his fifties named Bob Winfield, a former marine with a striking Marine Corps insignia tattooed on his right upper arm. He and Elias' grandad bonded immediately when they learned they'd both been in the armed forces. After the initial pleasantries, Bob disclosed the reason for his visit in some detail.

The old man shook his head ruefully. "My daughter came in one afternoon with the boy and said they were leaving the next day for Idaho. She claimed she'd found a job there and would be living with friends for a while until they got settled. Now, Dorothea is a bit of a wildcat and she doesn't listen to anybody's advice, so I wasn't gonna spend too much time trying to talk her out of it." He paused thoughtfully, as if to better recall the specifics.

"The boy just went along. He didn't seem too happy about the way things were going, but he's been around his mother long enough to know when it's best to shut your mouth and do as you're told. They spent the rest of that day packing, and first thing the following morning I dropped them off at the bus station and that was that. I had really started to enjoy having Elias around. When they first came to live with me, the boy was a handful, always looking to get in trouble. The last couple months, though, he was better behaved and seemed happier somehow."

"So, as far as you can tell she wasn't planning to come back this way?" Bob asked.

"I don't think so. They took most of their stuff . . . but you never know with these things. She left as unexpectedly as she showed up two years ago."

Chapter Twenty-Two

IT DIDN'T TAKE long for Laura to realize how much Elias' departure had affected Will. He became sullen and withdrawn, and despite his daily rehab sessions, it seemed like his progress had slowed, so he hadn't regained much more than an ability to shrug. Prior to that, he'd learned how to manipulate objects with his mouth, like a pen or a spoon. But all told, there was not much visible evidence of the wearying drives to Seven Pines. His therapists kept encouraging him to stick with it and initially he'd been able to keep his spirits up. But after Elias left, it was as if all the fervor and resilience had drained out of him.

Will continued to accompany Laura to school, but it was probably because he had nowhere else to go. He tried to maintain an even-keeled demeanor in the classroom, if only for the sake of the children. So he was taken aback one day when Elisa, a shy, chubby redhead with freckles came up to him and said matter-of-factly, "Mr. Will, are you still sad because of Elias?"

"Oh, no, not really. What makes you think so?" Will managed to say, despite being nonplussed.

"You look sad," she said, touching the back of his forearm with her little hand. "I know you can't feel me touching you, Mr. Will, but whenever my mommy touches me, I feel better. I hope this makes you feel better in your heart."

"Thank you, Elisa . . ." he said, as his voice choked with emotion.

Laura noticed the interaction and it piqued her curiosity. "So, what's up with you and Annie?" she whispered conspiratorially the next time they were alone together.

"Who?"

"Elisa. Doesn't she remind you of Annie—you know, from the movie?"

Will furrowed his brow briefly in concentration, then shook his head. "No, not really. Besides being a curly redhead with freckles, I don't see any similarities."

"Okay, anyway . . . so is she going to be your new best friend?"

Will smiled. "No, we're still working out the terms of the contract. She wanted to know if I was still sad because Elias left, which is surprising because I don't remember announcing to anyone that I was sad."

"You didn't need to," she said, "it was pretty obvious to everyone—except maybe you." Laura's mood brightened because Will was finally opening up about Elias.

"Well, Elias was a good kid. We had a good vibe going, till Ms. Crazy-Eyes came in and threatened to lift my head from off my shoulders. She's evil! No wonder the boy was so messed up."

Their conversation was light-hearted, the first of its kind since the confrontation with Ms. Mundy the previous week. Even the fact that Will had made direct reference to her for the first time since the episode was notable. As they talked, Laura mulled over the plan she had in mind for the weekend. She'd been racking her brains for something she could do to distract him and cheer him up when she remembered the many times that they'd talked about driving across the Chesapeake Bay Bridge-Tunnel. This impressive engineering feat spanned the mouth of the Chesapeake Bay, a little over seventeen and a half miles long. Beginning as a bridge at the shoreline, it transformed into a tunnel, disappearing underneath the ocean and reemerging briefly on the surface some distance from the shore, before dipping underwater and finally emerging as another bridge connecting to the shore on the other side.

The sight of bridges disappearing underwater and reappearing in the middle of the ocean was at once bewildering and inspiring, and while Will had never actually experienced it firsthand, the idea of it awed and captivated him from the time he was a boy. Before Laura, the only conversations he'd shared as an adult on the subject were with Mr. Fogarty, who viewed the engineering masterpiece as the work of the devil, referring to it abstrusely as Leviathan, the mythical sea monster of biblical lore. He believed its presence could only bring harm to the plant and animal life in the bay. From the time of its construction, he had watched its progress, hoping against hope it would never be completed—and his attitude towards it didn't mellow with time. Despite the old man's dark remonstrations, Will continued to be fascinated by the structure and resolved to take a drive on it one day, but so far that day hadn't come.

Laura was disquieted by the idea of traversing the bridge-tunnel, afraid she might lose control of her car on the high bridges or have an anxiety attack while driving through one of the tunnels in the middle of the ocean. She thought long and hard about it before she suggested the idea to Will, knowing that once she offered it up, she wouldn't be able to take it back.

Will's face lit up like a child's on Christmas Day when she brought up the subject. But a few minutes later, his enthusiasm was replaced by doubt. "Are you sure you'll be comfortable driving a van all that distance? It's almost eighteen miles all told, you know." Laura just sighed as Will continued, "And from all I've heard, the winds get pretty strong on the bridge, so you'd have to be steering the van through that."

"Yes, Will, I've thought about all that, but if you're that concerned, then maybe we should drop the plan. I thought you'd be more excited about it."

"I am, Laura, but I'm not the one who's going to be doing the driving. I just want to make sure that you're comfortable with the idea, because that's what matters most."

"I think I can do it," said Laura, suppressing any mention of her own concerns and self-doubt.

"Okay, then let's do it!" Will said, visibly brightening.

"Okay, then—we will!" Laura added energetically.

There was a brief pause, then Will spoke up again. "Er . . . just one thing, and I know it's not gonna happen but I'll say it anyway. What if you got to the other end of the bridge and weren't able to drive back because your nerves were shot? I wouldn't be able to help you with the driving."

Laura smiled awkwardly. "I already thought about that. If that happens, we'll just keep going up the Eastern Shore, then take the long way back through Maryland and DC via the I-95."

"Wow, so this might end up turning into a road trip. Okay, let's do it!" he said again, this time breaking out into a broad grin.

When the actual day came, Laura did a lot better than she thought she would. The sky was gray and overcast, and although it was noticeably breezy, she didn't have to wrestle with the steering wheel to keep the van moving in a straight line. Seagulls perched serenely atop the streetlights that formed a long row that lined the bridge and extended into the distance—until the bridge morphed into a tunnel and disappeared under the surface of the water. They were mostly silent during the ride, Will reveling in the scenery, while Laura kept a razor-sharp focus on the road ahead, as she drove hunched forward with an iron grip on the steering wheel.

As she kept pace with the slower procession of cars in the righthand lane, she tried hard to tune out the rambling discourse of a guest on a radio show who was upset about some esoteric bill passed in Richmond that he felt would spell ruin for the Tidewater area. His arguments were for the most part incoherent, and when the interviewer tried to cut him off, he resisted by simply continuing his rant at a higher volume. At about this time, they entered the first tunnel and lost the signal, so the radio noise was replaced by the equally distracting sound of static. Laura reproached herself for not turning off the radio earlier—before they reached the bridge—since now, as she drove through the tunnel, she didn't feel confident enough to take her hands off the wheel to reach for the knob and turn it off. So she gritted her teeth, resigned herself to the noise, and forged on.

As they emerged from the other end of the tunnel, she exhaled deeply. "One tunnel down, one more to go!" she announced, with a mixture of triumph and relief.

"You got this, babe, you got this!" Will said admiringly.

The annoying interview came back on the air as soon as they were out of the tunnel, and Laura immediately stretched out her hand towards the radio and pushed what she thought was the power knob, until she heard the sound of serene classical music fill the van. She was about to turn it off, but changed her mind. She listened for a few more seconds before she exclaimed, "Hey, that's Handel's *Largo from Xerxes!*"

"That's *what?*" Will asked, sounding flummoxed.

Laura had played the violin and piano through middle school and high school. At one point she'd considered studying music in college, but ultimately decided against it.

"It's one of my favorite pieces of music. You know who it reminds me of?"

"Who?"

"Keturah, your nurse at St. Matthew's."

"Who's Keturah? That's a weird name."

"Don't tell me you don't remember Keturah! She was the nurse who spent the most time with you. The short, chubby lady from Africa with a high-pitched voice and a gold stud in her nose . . . you don't remember?"

"Are you making this up?" Will asked, looking at her quizzically.

"No, I'm not making it up. You really don't remember Keturah?"

"Well, my memory is a bit fuzzy from that time, but I remember some of the nurses, including that linebacker dude they sent me after I chewed out one of them. But I think I would remember if I'd known someone with a name like Keturah."

"Hmm . . . I find that really odd. Well, she used to hum this melody all the time—and she had the most beautiful voice imaginable."

"The tune is very familiar, but I can't remember where I first heard it. And it does remind me of St. Matthew's, although I'm not sure why."

"Tunnel," Laura announced abruptly, indicating the need to suspend conversation as they entered the second tunnel.

The peaceful, airy music was replaced by static once again as they descended into the tunnel and proceeded wordlessly as before. Laura found herself struggling to understand how it was possible that Will had no memory of Keturah. By the time she'd left for Oklahoma, he'd regained consciousness. If he didn't remember the person he spoke to daily, then what else from that time had he said or done—seemingly in his right mind—that he might not have understood or intended, like when he'd told Laura he hated her.

As they climbed out of the tunnel, the music returned, but it was a different piece this time. Will seemed pensive as he listened to it.

"You know, I think I just remembered how I know that other song. When I was at St. Matthew's, I would have this recurring dream. I've never told anyone about it. It was not a bad dream—in fact, it was actually a very pleasant one. I would be out in an open field on a warm sunny day, running around barefoot, feeling the blades of grass tickling the soles of my feet. I remember feeling very happy. There was usually someone else with me, although I could never remember who it was when I woke up. And I think that's the song that was playing in my dream. Even when I woke up and realized I was still paralyzed and in a hospital bed, I would be pleased at the thought that at least I got to run around in my dreams."

"Hmm . . . that *is* interesting. You know what, when we get home, I'll check and see if I can find Keturah's number. It would be nice for you to talk with her. You'd probably remember her the minute you heard her pipsqueak voice. And she used to call you William—never Will—which nobody else does."

"It would certainly be nice to talk to her and thank her for taking care of me," Will agreed.

Chapter Twenty-Three

WHEN LAURA TELEPHONED St. Matthew's three days later, she spoke to Thomas Castillo, the manager on duty. His conversational manner was abrupt and businesslike, and he must have been on speakerphone because he sounded like he was inside a cave. Laura had never met or spoken with Mr. Castillo before, but his voice suddenly took on a tone of enthusiasm when she began describing Will.

"Of course, I remember Dr. Young. That was the young gentleman in Room C20 who was here last fall after a motor vehicle accident, right?"

Laura was a bit surprised he remembered Will with that level of detail. "Yes, that's him."

"How . . . how is your husband doing?" he said tentatively, sounding more subdued now, realizing her news might not be good.

"Oh, he's been doing alright. There've been struggles making the necessary adjustments, but he's been a trooper and he's making good progress."

"That's wonderful! I'm so glad to hear it. He was very sick when he went back to the hospital from here, and when he didn't return, we feared the worst. Is he at another facility now?"

"No, he came back home after the hospital."

"Really? That's amazing! I didn't think he'd be ready to go home for a while. I'll be sure to let my staff know—they'll be delighted to hear that. So, how may I be of assistance to you today, Mrs. Young?"

"I'm trying to get in touch with one of the nurses who took care of Will when he was at St. Matthew's. She moved to Oklahoma, and I was hoping you might have her contact information. Her name was Keturah."

"Keturah—of course! She was the nice lady from the islands with a bit of an accent."

"Well, yes . . . but I think she was from Africa."

"Got it. I know of only one Keturah, so we must be talking about the same person. I think she was a traveling nurse—not one of our permanent employees—but we probably still have her contact information. If I can't locate it in our records, I'll call her agency to get you what you need."

"Thank you. I'd really appreciate that," Laura said.

"Sure. And if you don't mind my asking . . . is there a reason you want to get in touch with her? Just in case the agency asks me, you know how these things go—there's nothing straightforward anymore these days."

"We just wanted to thank her for everything she did for us. Will especially wants to tell her that."

"Alright, sounds great! I'll get in touch with you once I find out. What's the best number to reach you at?"

Laura gave him her cell phone number, and then after thanking him again, she hung up.

A week went by, and she didn't hear from him. A few times she stopped short of calling him, overwhelmed with the urge to get the information she needed, but not wanting to pester him. He was probably a very busy man. During the time she waited, she said nothing to Will. He was aware that she intended to call the nursing facility, but didn't know she actually had called and was waiting for a reply.

She was sitting alone in the lobby at the Seven Pines rehab while Will had his therapy session. As her mind meandered peacefully her eyes started to close, until she was jolted awake by the buzzing sound in her handbag. Fumbling for her phone, she glanced at the number on the screen before answering nervously. "Hello?"

"Er . . . hello, is this Mrs. Young?"

"It is."

"Tom Castillo here, from St. Matthew's—we spoke last week. Sorry it took me so long to get back to you. When I reviewed our records, I discovered we didn't have Keturah's new contact information. I checked with some of the nurses who knew her, but they didn't have it either. I also spoke with her agency. Hannah—my contact person there—told me they had no record of someone by that name working with their agency, which makes no sense, because I remember Keturah very well; in fact, everyone here remembers her. Hannah promised to check again to make sure they hadn't misfiled her information, so I'm expecting a call back from her in a couple of days. I promise to do my best to get you what you need, Mrs. Young. I just wanted to update you now, so you didn't think I forgot about you."

"Thanks, Mr. Castillo, for all your good efforts and for keeping me posted," Laura replied, barely able to hide her disappointment.

As she stared at the blank wall on the opposite side of the lobby, trying to unpack the meaning of what she'd just been told, a thought suddenly crossed her mind. She remembered Keturah had called her before she left town, the last time they'd spoken. So she checked the record of previous calls on her cell, and immediately groaned in frustration as she recalled that she'd erased those as well as all her voicemails on a whim one day after Will was released from the hospital. "I can't believe I deleted her number! How could I?" she said aloud to herself, totally dismayed.

When Mr. Castillo called her two days later to inform her that the agency had no success in tracking down the information Laura had hoped to obtain, she was deeply disappointed but not entirely surprised since he hadn't sounded very hopeful in the last call. Still, as gracious and professional as he sounded, she was very perplexed at the idea that Keturah could vanish without a trace, and decided she would pay a visit to St. Matthew's one evening and talk directly to members of the nursing staff. She would have preferred to go alone, but since she couldn't leave Will home alone, she had to tell him what she'd been up to. In any case, the nurses would probably be excited to see him again, and know that their efforts in caring for him were not in vain.

Will didn't have a strong interest in finding Keturah, but he went along with Laura's plan to visit St. Matthew's, since all he had to do was accompany her. He also seemed somewhat irritated any time Laura pressed him to remember her, as if his inability to remember her indicated some brain damage from the accident that he was unwilling to acknowledge or confront.

When they arrived at the facility, they used the side door entrance that was equipped with a ramp. Normally there was someone at the reception desk to assist anyone needing information, but they must have stepped away for the moment. Laura's intention had been to ask for the nursing supervisor. Even if the supervisor hadn't met them during Will's time at the facility, they would be able to locate staff members who had—one of the highlights in a day at St. Matthew's was when a former patient came back to say 'Thank you.' They waited for a couple of minutes before Laura suggested they head down the hallway towards Will's old room, hoping they'd run into someone they recognized.

"It feels strange wandering around this place," she mused, "hoping we'll see someone familiar . . ."

"Is that you, Mrs. Young?" said a cheerful voice behind them.

Laura turned around. It was Grace, one of the nurse's aides who'd helped with Will's care a number of times.

"Oh, and Dr. Young, you look so good! I'm so happy to see you!" Grace was a woman in her sixties who exuded energy and ebullience. She immediately reached across Will's chest with one arm and pressed her face next to his in an impulsive show of affection. Since she was a little less than five feet tall, she wasn't much taller than Will seated in his powerchair.

"It's so nice of you to come and visit!" she said, turning to Laura. "Tom, our manager, told us last week that he'd spoken with you and that Dr. Young was doing fine, but it's still a pleasant surprise to see you again. Come with me to the break room so you can say hello to the others."

Delighted by the idea, the two followed Grace down the hallway.

"Hey, everyone, we have a special visitor who's come to see us!" she announced jubilantly as she stepped into the room, holding the door open for Will.

As he peered into the room, he realized there probably wasn't enough room for his powerchair to fit, since there were some chairs and a table clustered near the door. "You go inside," Will told Laura. "Then I'll steer my chair into the doorway without going all the way inside."

Grace was still holding the door open as Laura entered, and Will maneuvered the wheelchair into the doorway so he was partially inside the room. The wheelchair stopped the door from closing, so Grace could let go. There were six staff members inside. They'd been sitting around a table cluttered with two uneaten slices of a pepperoni pizza surrounded by paper plates, soda cans and Styrofoam coffee cups.

"Is that you Dr. Young?" one of the nurses called out from the far end of the table. "You don't remember me, but I took care of you when you were here. My name is Trevor. Hello, Mrs. Young!"

"Hi, Trevor. Of course, I remember you," Laura replied warmly. "Will, do you remember Trevor?"

"As a matter of fact, I do. I also remember that gentleman over there. You were my respiratory therapist, although I don't remember your name."

"Samir," replied the old man, beaming.

All the other faces in the room looked somewhat familiar, but Laura didn't know their names since they'd not been as deeply or as frequently involved in Will's care.

"Where's the big guy, the football player?" asked Will.

"Who—Joe B?" Trevor asked.

"Yeah, I think that might have been his name."

"He's not working tonight," Trevor said.

"Wow, you're looking pretty good for the shape you left us in, Dr. Young!" observed one of the orderlies named Spencer, erupting with raucous laughter.

"Yup, that's true. I was there the night they took you to the hospital," another one named Trina interjected. "You looked like you were fixing to leave this world."

Will smiled. "Thank you all for everything you did for me."

Amidst the big smiles and approving murmurs that followed, Laura spoke. "Would any of you happen to have Keturah's contact information? I was hoping to get in touch with her."

Trevor shook his head. "Tom asked us for it last week, and for some reason nobody took down her number when she left. She was a great nurse and an exceptional human being!"

"Hear, hear," Jim murmured in agreement. He was another one of the nurses who knew Will.

"I just find it odd that she seems to have vanished without a trace," Laura opined. "I even checked the website of the state nursing board in Oklahoma and looked her up, but found nothing. I googled her name as well and came up empty-handed. You all remember her, so I know she wasn't a figment of my imagination. I say that because Will doesn't remember her at all. But recently we heard a song on the radio that she used to hum all the time, and he associates that melody with a recurrent dream he used to have only when he was here."

A perplexed silence ensued.

"You know," Trevor observed, "I remember her singing. In fact, a couple of times I asked her if she'd ever considered a singing career. But you know Keturah—she just laughed it off. Who knows, maybe she changed her name and embarked on a career in the performing arts. Maybe that's why we can't find her."

Samir hadn't said much, which was quite usual for him and what everyone expected. So when he cleared his throat to speak, everyone turned in his direction, looking a bit surprised.

"Maybe she was angel," he stated without hesitation.

That evoked a few confused expressions, partly related to what he said, and partly related to the fact that he spoke at all. If anyone had been expecting him to elaborate, then they didn't know Samir, for he had said all that needed to be said. Laura's eyes met his, and a strange tingling sensation went through her as she reflected on his words. Samir, for his part, was thinking about how Keturah reminded him of his late daughter Safiya, and how, when she told him she was leaving, he'd felt as if he had finally been given the opportunity to say a proper goodbye to Safiya.

"Well, there you have it, folks!" Spencer bellowed. "Either she was an angel, an aspiring celebrity or one heck of an illegal alien! Any way you look at it, Keturah—she was the best!"

"Hear, hear," echoed Jim, "nothing but the best!"

Chapter Twenty-Four

WILL JERKED HIS head and grimaced, then pushing out his lower lip, blew a strong puff of breath upward towards his face, launching the annoying fly back into the air. He knew the willful and impetuous creature would be back in short order to find another place on his face to land. This sort of thing had never been an issue for him in the past, when he had full use of his arms and could mindlessly swat away a fly without being distracted from whatever else he was doing or thinking.

His eyes went to a group of about ten teenagers who were playing a spirited game of left-leg soccer in the sand. From the appearance of things, they were all right-footed—and probably not exceptional players to start with—but they were having the time of their lives, hooting and screeching with laughter, to the amusement of the beachgoers nearby who were basking lazily in the sun. It was about one o'clock in the afternoon, and families were still making their way onto the sand, carrying folding chairs, giant beach umbrellas and tote bags stuffed with towels and colorful plastic toys.

Will felt happy and peaceful whenever he came here—sitting on the boardwalk on a summer's day, watching the waves tumbling onto the shore, surrounded by hundreds of people lazing around, having temporarily disengaged themselves from their everyday worries. Whenever the weather was good and the opportunity presented itself, this was the one place he always felt drawn to. In a way, he'd become a little like Mr. Fogarty, although without his intense anxiety about sea levels, and the impact of Leviathan on the bay and all the underwater creatures. For Will, the ocean was a source of meditative calm, where he could tune his mind to the rhythmic booming of the waves interlaced with the joyous cries of the sea gulls. Mr. Fogarty's relationship with the ocean involved keeping a constant vigil at the beach, always on the lookout for potential threats. Because of that, he probably never experienced the pure pleasure of just being there and enjoying the ocean for what it was.

"Sir?"

An unfamiliar male voice interrupted his serene reflections. He looked up, somewhat startled. Before him was a lean, muscular man in his late twenties wearing sunglasses, beach shorts and flip-flops. Will also noticed a large tattoo on the inside of his right forearm. Clutching his right hand was a young girl about six years old. Will stared at him blankly.

"Yes?"

"Aren't you Mr. Will?"

"I am. And you are?"

The man slid his sunglasses over the top of his head, and addressing the little girl said, "Abby, run along and catch up with your mom. I'll be right there. Here, take your bucket and shovel. You can go and start working on your sandcastle."

Will was still puzzled. Even with the sunglasses off, there was nothing familiar about him.

"Sir, I can tell you don't remember me, but you used to come to my school when I was a kid. Your wife, Mrs. Young, was my teacher . . ."

Will studied his face, then slowly shook his head in disbelief. "Elias? Is that you?"

"Yes, sir. It's me. When I saw you sitting here, I thought I was dreaming. For all the years that have elapsed since then, I fervently hoped I would see you again. My wife makes fun of me because every time I see a black man in a wheelchair, I make up an excuse to get a good look at him just to make sure it's not you. When I saw you just now, I knew it was my lucky day, because you look exactly like I remember you."

"Wow, Elias! It's been quite a few years since I last saw you," marveled Will.

"Twenty years, sir."

"So where have you been? What have you been up to?"

"Well, that right there is my family," Elias said, pointing to a woman with two children, who were weaving through the throng of people to get close to the water. "That's my wife Josie and my two kids—Abby, who was just here, and Danny, the older one. She's six and he's eight. We just moved to the area about a year ago for my job. I'm in the navy."

"Really?" Will exclaimed, clearly impressed. "I always wondered what happened to you after you left with your mom."

The joyful expression on Elias' face faded a little, and his voice took on an almost somber tone. "That was a very difficult time in my life, sir. I'm sorry about the way my mother yelled at you. She'd been wrestling with her demons ever since my father left us. I don't remember much about him. They'd both been addicted to pain pills, and after he left, she spent all her time and energy looking for whatever high she could find. Most of the time she was at home, she was either strung out on dope or raging mad, raging at everyone. I actually preferred it when she was high, because she would leave me alone." Elias sighed deeply before he went on.

"When we were staying at my granddaddy's place, she used to say she had a migraine, and go straight to our bedroom when she came home from work so she could get high. My granddaddy—God love him—kept telling her to see a doctor if the migraines were such a problem. I don't think he ever figured out what she was doing. She threatened me, saying if I ever told him she would kill me, and I believed her. You saw my mom—she was crazy—I thought she would carry out her threat. So, I just kept my mouth shut."

"So where did you go after you left Norfolk?" Will asked.

"We went to Idaho. My mom said she had a friend there we could stay with who she'd talked to before we left; although when we got there, it seemed like they didn't know her too well. They might have been in school together. I heard my mom say we were going there to get away from people like you, if you know what I'm saying . . . I think that's how we ended up there. Anyway, the lady allowed us to stay a couple of days, and then told us we were on our own. We found an apartment, and my mom got a job at a hardware store. Things settled down for a while, but then she started using drugs more and more, and one day she got arrested. I got home from school one day and a neighbor who heard me came out and told me what had happened." He paused for a few beats to catch his breath.

"Anyway, I ended up in the foster care system, which was basically hell—living with strange people who felt they had the right to tell me how to live my life just because they let me stay at their house for a little while. I got kicked out of a couple of schools for fighting, and would probably have ended up dead or in jail had it not been for a military recruiter who showed up at my high school in my senior year. From the minute he started talking to me, I knew it was for me. I liked everything I heard about it—the structure, the discipline and being a part of something bigger than myself, things that, for the most part, I had never had in my life. Joining the navy was the best thing I ever did!"

As Elias spoke, Will's gaze drifted to the tattoo on his right forearm. In artistic block letters, seamlessly joined together, it read

JER2911. His brow furrowed, as he tried to figure out what it meant, when Elias noticed where Will's attention was focused.

"That's for my best friend Lavon Antony, who died in a helicopter crash—he had one just like this. He and three other guys went out on a routine helicopter run one morning, and then—just like that—the bird fell out of the sky, and they were all gone. He and I started boot camp at the same time, and we became buddies when we found out we were both from North Carolina—he was from Ahoskie, and my family is from Kill Devil Hills, which is where my mom and I lived before moving to Virginia.

"Lavon was the coolest guy; he never panicked and never ever got stressed out. He used to recite a verse from the Bible— Jeremiah 29:11—and he quoted it so often that most of the guys in our platoon knew it by heart. 'For I know the plans I have for you,' he would say, 'plans to prosper you and not to harm you, plans to give you a hope and a future.' You should have seen the look of surprise on the chaplain's face during Lavon's funeral, when he started to read the verse and about fifty guys started reciting it out loud, including some of the roughest guys in the platoon. In fact, by the time he died, most of the people on the base had no idea who Lavon was—they all knew him as Jeremiah. The tattoo suited him well because he always showed up willing to help and knew the right thing to say, so we all read it as 'Jeremiah to 9-1-1.' His death hit me hard—we'd become like brothers by that time, we hung out together all the time." Elias stopped for a minute and seemed to be holding back tears.

"I visited his parents once after we moved here. We'd never met before, and they were kind of stiff and formal because there's not a lot of white guys who come out to where they live; and the last one who came was the one who brought them the news that he'd died. Once I took my jacket off and his mom saw the tattoo, it was a completely different story! She started bawling and hugging me, almost as if I was her son who had come back to life. She said the verse was the one thing everyone in town remembered about Lavon, from the time he was in middle school."

Elias glanced briefly in the direction of his family. His son was wading in the water, about knee deep, and his daughter was kneeling in the wet sand, trying to build a sandcastle.

"How's Mrs. Young?" he asked, turning back to Will.

A doleful look appeared on Will's face, and his eyes began to glisten. He started to say something but stopped momentarily, unable to continue. Then, resolutely, he spoke in a voice barely above a whisper. "She was a fine person. I couldn't have asked for anyone better. It's a shame it took me so long to figure that out. She always supported me and never once complained, even when I took her for granted. I miss her so much!" His voice was quivering, and the tears had started trickling down his face. He collected himself before he continued.

"One day we came to the beach . . . a day just like today. She went back to our car because she forgot her phone. I thought I heard a screech of tires, but I wasn't really sure. Anyway, after about a half-hour passed and she hadn't come back, I started getting worried. I tried calling her phone, but she wasn't picking up. Then Mr. Ahmad, the guy from the ice cream shop at the corner across from the parking lot came looking for me—he was used to seeing us frequently, coming and going. He'd recognized Laura, and as the ambulance took her away, he realized I was probably out here with no way of knowing what had happened and no one to help me. The police had the car keys since they'd been knocked out of her hand. Mr. Ahmad explained to them that I was here with no way to get home, so they gave him the keys. He drove me home in the van and called my parents. I'm eternally grateful to him for being there for me. I stop by his store to say hello every time I come here.

"Since the funeral, I come here almost every day when the weather is good. I can still feel her presence when I'm here. I have a personal caregiver called Lakeisha, who's probably watching us right now. She takes care of me and drives me wherever I need to go. She's a part-time jiujitsu instructor, by the way, a vocation I find rather fascinating. And, as a matter of fact, I think she did a few years in the navy. I haven't figured out why she'd want to spend her days with someone like me when there are so many other jobs available to her, probably for more pay, but I'm not complaining—she's perfect for me. When I'm here, she knows I need to spend time with Laura, so she parks my wheelchair in my favorite spot and hangs around at a considerate distance. If I need her, I just call her. Watch this!"

Will raised his extended right arm clumsily, and brought it across to a touch screen attached to the left arm piece of his wheelchair. With the base of his thumb, he tapped on the telephone icon labeled "Lakeisha" and the phone dialed once before being picked up.

"Yes, Dr. Young . . ." A female voice could be heard on the speakerphone.

"Hey, Lakeisha, I just wanted to introduce my friend Elias. We go back a long way. He was Laura's student many years ago." He looked up at Elias and said, "Look around those benches back there and you'll see Lakeisha waving."

An athletic black woman in sunglasses, wearing a purple spaghetti-strap top and denim shorts waved from one of the benches about a hundred feet away. Elias waved back. She nodded in acknowledgment, then hung up the phone.

Elias eyes suddenly opened wide in surprise. "Wait a minute . . . you moved your arm!" he said incredulously.

Will grinned. "I thought you'd never notice! I did several months of physical therapy and it paid off—I can raise my arm and tap my screen. I can even hold up a sixteen-ounce soda cup with both arms and drink through a straw, which is pretty good considering how I started out. I still can't swat a fly because I don't move fast enough, and I end up banging myself in the face. And I can't pick things up with my fingers, and likely never will—but that's okay."

"Wow! So, what happened to the straw? You know—the one you used to blow into so the wheelchair could move."

"Oh, I upgraded to a touch screen and this little joystick here, as soon as I was able to use my arms."

Elias shook his head slowly in amazement. There was a joyous smile on his face, that was gradually replaced by a more somber expression. He began hesitantly, "How long has it been since . . ."

"She died seven years ago."

A long pause ensued, with each man lost in his private ruminations. The silence was not the awkward type that needed to be drowned out with mindless conversation; it was a calm, reflective space inhabited by two people who were perfectly comfortable in each other's presence.

After a few moments, Elias' phone started ringing. It was his wife. "Mr. Will, I've got to go now. I'm so glad I ran into you! I've dreamed of this day for many years. Let me take down your number, so I don't have to wait another twenty years to see you again."

Elias hastily entered Will's number into his phone and texted his contact information back to him, then hurriedly descended the stairs to the beach to catch up with his family. As Will watched him go—tall, confident and composed—he felt a warmth come over him as he remembered the chaotic hell-bound child from many years before.

Then his thoughts wandered back to the lovely Laura, and he smiled as the tears started to well up in his eyes . . . life was good after all.

PRAISE FOR THE BOOK

"A moving testament to the importance of our connections to each other, *Ten Thousand Rocks* illuminates how adversity can spur resilience in life and in love." *BookLife Reviews, Editor's Pick*

"Githaiga, a practicing physician, is a shrewd writer who contrasts the sterility of the medical world with the messiness of human emotion." *Kirkus Reviews*

". . . a book that will make you think about life, its choices, and the important things that surround you each day." *San Francisco Book Review*

". . . a reflective novel about the price of greed—and the rewards of kindness and perseverance." *Foreword Clarion Reviews*

". . . a summary of life encounters that is compellingly presented and thought-provokingly analyzed." *Midwest Book Review*

ABOUT THE AUTHOR

NDIRANGU GITHAIGA was born in Kenya and immigrated to the United States. He is a practicing physician based in Virginia. Visit www.ndirangugithaiga.com to learn more.

Follow Ndirangu at:
Facebook: https://www.facebook.com/ndirangu.githaiga.9/
Instagram: https://www.instagram.com/ndirangu.githaiga